The Healer & The Warlord

Kelsey Winton

Contents

To the girl who never stopped fighting, even when no one saw her battle—may you always get to choose your own fate.

"Once the thread of fate is tangled, it cannot be undone."

-Kikyo, *Inuyasha*

A Note on Piracy

While piracy may be an exciting theme in stories, it's important to support authors by obtaining books through legitimate means.

If you're having trouble accessing a copy of *The Healer and the Warlord*, or if you find yourself reading a pirated copy, please reach out to me directly at authorkelseywinton@gmail.com. I'm more than happy to assist you in finding the right way to enjoy the book.

Thank you for your support!

Blurb

Their bond was fated by the gods, but their love must be earned.

In a land ruled by gods and bound by fate, Runa bears the healing blessing of the Iyashite, a gift from the Goddess of Life.

Her magic is sacred, powerful and dangerously coveted. When she's captured and brought before Keshin, the brutal warlord blessed by the God of War, her fate changes in an instant. The gods forge a divine bond between them, tying their destinies together.

But to Runa, this connection is no gift. It's a life sentence chaining her to a mindless brute.

Despite her reluctance, Keshin and Runa must face the difficulties of battle together. And the more she sees what lies beneath the warlord's armor, the more Runa is drawn to Keshin's unexpected honor.

As they navigate fragile truces, looming threats, and the mysterious ways their powers intertwine, Runa must decide whether to defy the gods or embrace their will. And whether the man fate bound to her might just be the one her heart chooses.

Chapter 1

Runa didn't appreciate being ripped away from healing someone in the middle of the battle. Nor did she appreciate being
bound and dragged away from the people of Sakanoue, who would
suffer over the greed of these lords. What were a few lives of innocents
compared to gaining land?

Granted, trying to heal the wounded in the middle of a raging battle
wasn't Runa's best idea.

Sounds of the ongoing battle raged in the distance as men forced
her to walk away. Runa bit her tongue to stop the tears from rolling
down her face. Her heart ached for the townspeople caught in this
brutal conflict.

"Don't worry Iyashite, we'll take you somewhere safe," one of her
captors said.

She hated that title, Iyashite. It meant, "divine healer" and was a reminder of Alyis's goddess-given gift—one for which Runa did not ask.

And she was the only one in all of Oshiren with that title. The only one in all the land divinely blessed by the Goddess of Life to magically heal. Because of her gift, she was hunted by various lords from all over the land. They wanted her powers for themselves, to keep her like a doll.

Her healing powers weren't meant to be hoarded by one man though. She was meant to help those who could not help themselves—like the people back in Sakanoue.

Instead, when these two men found her using her divine powers, they restrained her, bound her, and took her away from the village, presumably to one of the two warring lords.

What if these two warlords were fighting over her? Word could have gotten out that she was in Sakanoue, and these warlords might have sent their armies to retrieve her. When she heard the armies were coming, Runa chose to stay in Sakanoue to help those in need.

Guilt squeezed her heart. If she had left, the warlords might have followed her and left the people alone. How many people died because of her choice?

Runa's life was an ironic juxtaposition. She was like a scroll, and death was the ink that seeped through her and smudged every name she tried to save.

She shook her head. There was no time for thoughts like that. Besides, according to the townspeople, these two rulers had been disputing over land, and this village was where that conflict had boiled over.

The camp reeked of metal and blood. Runa was no stranger to warcamps, but this was the largest one she'd seen. Her captors bound her hands then led her between tents, feet squishing in the mud.

Based on the banners painted with Tharaveld's holy symbol of a fist clutching a sword, the Senshin's men had found her. The warlord and ruler of the Tensho providence was divinely blessed by Tharaveld, the God of War. Her mind turned over every rumor she'd ever heard: the warlord with fire in his blood, a man who cleaved through armies as if they were wheat. Above all else, he was Tharaveld's chosen.

What few soldiers remained stood at attention, spears ready, eyes sharp, assessing her. No doubt wondering what she was doing there. They passed the infirmary, the groans of injured men echoed around Runa while attendants darted around with bloodied strips of cloth.

She had no doubt she'd be there soon enough, helping heal the survivors. That is, if this Senshin didn't want to use her for something else.

They approached the center of the camp, moving toward a larger tent set apart from the rest. The Senshin's tent, she assumed.

"We found the Iyashite," one of her captors addressed the soldiers tasked to guard the fabric.

She watched, unimpressed, as the guards' eyes widened and looked her over.

"You sure it's her?" the guard asked.

"I watched her use her power myself," her captor nodded.

The guard pulled back the tent flaps and waited for her. With her head held high, she entered. Inside lanterns cast dim light on the large table dominating the space. It was covered with maps, goblets, and tiny figurines. Shelves of scrolls lined the cloth walls, and there seemed to be another room to her right, probably personal quarters

"You'll be safe here, Iyashite," one of her captors said.

Runa stifled a laugh. Safe was a funny word coming from the people who kidnapped her and dragged her into the Senshin's warcamp.

But she didn't say anything. Instead, she straightened her spine and lifted her chin, ready to face whatever this Senshin wanted with her.

Runa had never met another divinely blessed individual. There were only six of them, one for each of the six gods. She prepared herself for a monster, fire-eyed cloaked in blood, and instead she met the eyes of a man whose presence crackled like the moment before lightning strikes.

Caught in his gaze, she didn't know how much time passed. Distantly she noted murmuring before the tent flaps opened and more people filed into the tent. It didn't matter how many people filled the room, as one single figure dominated the space.

There was no mistaking the Senshin. It wasn't just his tall, imposing form that filled the tent with irrefutable command. That was secondary compared to the undeniable aura radiating from him that sent shivers through her body. His eyes burned a sanguine red, shining with a divine power that she had no doubt he channeled during the recent battle.

"My Lord Senshin, we found the Iyashite," her captor said with a bow.

Runa could not tear her eyes away from the Senshin, telling herself it was because, like her, he was divinely blessed. In a way, he was her mirror. Where she healed people, he killed them.

His yoroi armor was made from crimson lacquered, rectangular plates of dark steel and wood connected by leather laces. There were no decorative flourishes, no ornamental tassels, just the symbol of Tharaveld on his chest. A dark liquid splattered the armor. Blood, Runa assumed, proof of the lives he'd taken.

He wore no helmet, revealing shoulder length dark hair pulled back in a ponytail. His face was haunted by countless battles. Each scar a story of another victory.

His gaze raked over her, not lewdly, not cruelly, but thoroughly. As if she were a storm on the horizon he studied to determine if it would bring rain or ruin.

Then his eyes lifted to hers, and he looked into her, steadily and unyielding with the unmistakable weight of a man who already knew she would change everything.

Vaguely, Runa registered other figures filing into the tent after him, other officers or individuals in his command. The Senshin, however, continued to hold her gaze, as if he was unable to look away.

After what felt like an eternity, he did something surprising.

He bowed to her, causing the men around him to do the same.

"Honorable Iyashite," he said.

His voice wasn't as threatening as she expected. Sure, it was low and rough with an edge of command but it felt more like a quiet force settling over her, like the distant promise of an incoming storm.

The men remained in their kneeling position, waiting for her to acknowledge them. They'd be waiting a while. Runa did not speak, nor did she return the bow. She would not bend to these men.

Eventually the Senshin straightened and looked to her captors. "Your efforts in finding and escorting the Iyashite here will be rewarded."

He turned to another man to his right. "Hoshi, see to it."

The man, Hoshi, stepped forward, his salt and pepper hair catching in the light, his sharp gaze lingering on her. "This way." The command was soft and his presence reminded Runa of a steady stone against the waves.

"I regret the manner of your arrival. But you are safe here, and no one will harm you," he addressed Runa again.

The Senshin closed the distance between them, approaching Runa with smooth, deliberate moves. As if she were a wounded animal, easily spooked. He wasn't entirely wrong. Runa's heart thundered in her chest, every instinct telling her to run away. But that would be a foolish effort in the middle of the Senshin's warcamp. She wouldn't get two feet before they'd recaptured her.

"Allow me. No one who bares Aylis's light should be treated like a prisoner," Senshin said as if her dignity mattered to him.

It wasn't an apology, but it felt like the closest thing someone like him could offer.

Her bindings weren't tight, but they had left faint indentations in her skin. He reached for the knots at her wrists, hands steady and sure despite the battle-worn calluses that brushed her skin. His touch was gentle, almost reverent, as he loosened the cords. Runa didn't flinch.

She studied his face, his dark eyes, serious, unreadable, and fixed on the knots. His fingers moved with care as he undid the cords. As the rope slipped free, she raised her arms to her chest, rubbing her wrists with care. Runa channeled a little of Aylis's power, soothing the irritation.

Maybe it was their close proximity, or maybe it was because Runa had activated her power, but only then did she notice a puncture wound in the Senshin's shoulder just under his armor.

Good, she thought. He deserved that, and so much more. She tried not to think about all the wounded innocents she could be helping while they held her captive.

More silence passed between them, as if he was waiting for her to speak. Runa would not. She was still skeptical of this man and his motives.

"Our paths crossed for a purpose. You may begin your healing with this wound." This time the Senshin commanded her.

Runa couldn't help it, she sputtered out a laugh. She quickly covered her mouth, she knew she shouldn't laugh at him. If the Senshin considered her disrespect a great offense, he could have her killed.

He had probably killed for less.

But this man thought she would jump at the chance to obey him. What a fool.

She never took orders well.

The Senshin stood, expressionless in front of her, still as the great trees that surrounded the camp. His men, however, shifted nervously, their eyes darting between their lord and her.

"What is humorous?" the Senshin asked.

Aylis help her, this time she snorted as she chortled. His request was ridiculous.

"No," Runa said as she got herself under control.

"No?" the Senshin repeated, raising a single eyebrow.

"You send your soldiers into a defenseless village, hunt me down, bind me, and drag me here, all so you can demand I heal you?" she asked, her palms pressed together like a prayer.

Was it the smartest idea to challenge the Senshin? No. But she was betting that the men in this room desired her healing abilities enough to tolerate her tongue.

So Runa held her head high and met the Senshin's gaze. She would not back down from this tyrant.

A man to the side of the Senshin spoke, "Honorable Iyshite—"

"Don't call me that."

The man shifted his weight but continued, "It would be in your best interest—"

"Don't waste your breath. The answer is no."

The other bystanders in the room whispered to themselves, probably shocked at her bold refusal.

"This is not a request," the Senshin spoke again.

Runa snorted. "Of course it is."

The Senshin pursed his lips, irritated. Runa knew he wanted an explanation. But she refused to give him one. She didn't owe him anything.

"You think you can make me do anything you want with a simple command?" Runa asked.

He did not break his gaze with her as he again commanded, "You will heal me."

He didn't get it. Runa pretended to think about it for a moment, tilting her head to the side, before she again answered. "No."

"I will—"

"What? Kill me?" Runa asked. "Go ahead."

Thankfully, the brute just stood there. So Runa felt empowered to keep going. "You know who I am; that's why you sought me out. You know I work tirelessly to heal the injured in the wake of men like you." Each word she spoke was more irate than the last. "You have so little respect for life. Since the moment Aylis blessed me, I've done whatever she's called me to do. But there is no way I will ever heal a monster like you."

The Senshin stepped closer to her, crowding her vision until it appeared there was nothing in the room but the two of them. Tension-filled seconds passed as his eyes narrowed, assessing.

Runa was shocked when the next thing out of his mouth was a laugh. Something deep from his stomach. He stepped away from her to pace the width of the table. After a moment, the other men in the room laughed with him.

She shifted uncomfortably.

After what felt like several minutes, the Senshin stopped laughing, then he stalked back toward Runa.

"I did not come for you," he said.

Runa didn't believe him. "Then why am I here?"

When she opened her mouth to speak, her tongue tingled similar to the way her hands did when she channeled Aylis's divine energy. She had never felt it on her tongue before.

There were stories. Legends of how only the will of the gods passed through the tongue. Their divine commands. When they created a holy bond, an Unmei.

Fear raced up her spine. She had to get out of there.

Please, Aylis, she begged her goddess in silent prayer, *anyone but him.*

Runa slammed her lips together. Maybe, if she didn't open her mouth, the power couldn't escape and Runa would be safe from another divine intervention. Aylis couldn't want this for her, could she?

The tingling sensation spread from her tongue to her lips, begging her to open, to let the energy out. The tingling turned into pain, and still she did not open her mouth.

Gripping her chin between her thumbs and forefinger, the Senshin tilted her head up to look him in the eye.

"Don't," he said.

Clearly, a man of many words. Still, Runa understood. He didn't want her to fight it. She watched, transfixed, as a bright white light danced in his mouth. Whatever was happening between them, he wasn't resisting. Unlike her, there was no panic on his face.

With surprising gentleness, he used the pad of his thumb to lower her bottom lip, pulling it down, and she could not bear the pain any longer, acquiescing to him and opening her mouth. His touch was careful in a way she wasn't used to. Usually, her patients desperately grabbed onto her like they were clinging to life. Not him. He touched her like he was holding the world's most precious treasure.

A matching divine white energy leaped from her mouth to intertwine with his. It started as two pieces of thread winding around one another until it created a single strand. Soon, the circumference grew to encompass both of them within the light.

Typically, Aylis's power was like a warm, comforting hug. Not this time. Runa felt a fire burning through her, burning the rope and freeing her hands, but not harming them.

The Senshin took her left hand in his to raise it between them. A vibrant red line, fine as a silk thread, appeared on both of their hands.

It wrapped down their ring fingers, twirling like the dancing lights encircling them. Then it looped between their forefingers and thumbs and to their palms and back around to make another full circle around their wrists where it tied into an infinity knot just below the back of their hands.

The Senshin held their hands up, admiring the new marks inked into their skin.

"Unmei," a soldier muttered in awe.

"The mark of the fated," another said.

All hit their knees, bowing before the two of them. No, no, no—she did not want this. *Aylis, what are you thinking?* Runa wondered. An Unmei mark meant that by the will of the gods, they were irrevocably tied together.

Runa pulled against the Senshin's grip. "Let me go, you bastard."

"Keshin," he said.

Runa paused.

"It is my name," he clarified. "You will use it."

Keshin did not release their joined hands. She looked at him expectantly, waiting to see what he wanted.

The deafening silence continued until she realized he wanted her name as well.

"Runa," she muttered.

"Runa," he repeated in a low gravel voice that sent shivers right to her core. "I vow, here and now, with Tharaveld as my witness, to always keep you safe."

Runa felt the weight of his words in her chest. But she didn't trust them.

Then he ordered various men in the room to return to the village, procure clothing for her, and bring it back to his tent.

Panic set in. Did he expect her to sleep with him?

"Absolutely not," Runa protested.

The room fell silent.

"If the gods' will bind us together, I will remain in your camp for now. But I will not sleep in your bed like your consort."

Keshin's gaze burned into her, as if he was determining how serious she was. Eventually, he nodded once and ordered another tent next to his be repurposed for her use.

Runa wasn't thrilled at the idea of being so close, but she didn't protest. Logically, she knew being next to the divinely blessed warlord—and now her bonded partner—would be the safest place for her. But she didn't have to like it.

Her mind drifted back to his vow. Keshin wasn't the kind of man who spoke lightly. His words were forged like blades, meant to endure. But that didn't quiet the voice in her head whispering, *how long until someone tries to rip it all away again? How long until another warlord came chasing power and tore through everything she hadn't even chosen? And what would she do then? Bleed for another man's ambition?*

The silence of the tent was suffocating, too still, too full of all the things she couldn't scream. Her life had been torn away like parchment burned at the edges. She hadn't gotten to say goodbye to anything. Not the soft rhythms of temple work. Not the quiet dignity of her own path. Not the simple, foolish dream of being free.

Her hands trembled in her lap before she clenched them tight. A sharp breath. A hot tear. She didn't even remember when she started crying. It's just that the ache in her chest wouldn't stop growing, blooming with every beat of her heart like a wound refusing to close.

Was she meant to be grateful? To smile sweetly and say "thank you" for a fate she hadn't chosen—again?

Runa looked down at the red mark, the divine thread that tethered her to a warlord she barely knew. It pulsed faintly against her skin like a living thread. A brand. A binding. A curse.

Fine, she thought. If this was the path they carved for her then she would walk it. But she'd do it with her eyes open and her head held high.

It was futile to try and defy the will of the gods. But Runa damn well wanted to try.

Chapter 2

I t felt like months had passed since Runa joined Keshin's war camp. It had been one week. By the end of the seventh day, Runa's patience had been whittled down to splinters and she had to get out of the camp, if only for the day.

First, there was Keshin's overprotective nature. At least he followed through on his promise to give her her own tent—right next to his.

Then, he assigned two female attendants who were instructed to attend to the Iyashite's every need. So now she had these women bowing before her asking what she needed thousands of times a day. What she really wanted was for them to leave her alone. She never had attendants before and could bathe and dress herself, thank you very much.

And she couldn't forget about the guards stationed outside of her tent every hour of the day and night. Runa swore they were assigned to make sure she didn't leave her own tent. The only place she was permitted to go was the medical tent with escorts, of course.

Every time she left the tent people stared at her. It was rare enough to meet one person blessed by the gods. Having two in one camp was unheard of. Two blessed, brought together by the will of the gods themselves. This was a legend in the making to onlookers.

Of course it would happen to her. It wasn't enough to be blessed by a god. No, her goddess also wanted to play matchmaker. It was fine. When someone eventually killed Keshin, she'd be free—probably. It wasn't like there were books on how this kind of bond worked, just legends that the Unmei existed.

Unfortunately, as of now, Keshin was still breathing, so life would go on as it was.

She spent most of the week healing injured soldiers before returning to her tent where someone brought her meals and took care of her chamber pot.

If Aylis wanted her bonded to Keshin, then Runa would accept that. But she could not spend another minute in this camp with Keshin trying to control everything.

Today, she resolved to return to the village of Sakanoue to check on the wounded and injured. Runa awoke before her attendants entered to poke and prod at her, and donned her traveling clothes. She had a plan and every precious second counted.

Once dressed, Runa packed a traveling bag with bundles of her herbs, making a mental note that she needed more white willow bark.

With her things gathered, she stood and took a moment to collect herself before taking a breath and storming out of the tent. She needed to put some distance between herself and her two armed shadows. Keshin may have learned he couldn't order her to do as he wished, but he could still command the people around her.

She only made it ten steps before the armed shadows realized she was leaving and followed her.

"Honorable Iyashite," Shadow One called after her, jogging to catch up. She could hear their yoroi clanking as they moved.

"It's Runa," she said.

"This isn't the way to the medical tent," Shadow Two said.

"Great observation."

She needed to move faster. Picking up her pace, she navigated through the camp, dodging people, soldiers, horses, supply wagons, and tents.

From the little she saw, Runa understood how the camp was laid out. Like spokes on a wheel, Keshin's tent was the central hub. Surrounding him were his commanding officers' tents, followed by the medics and quartermasters' tents and supply wagons. Soldiers stayed in the outermost ring, along with slapdash training areas filled with polearms and axes. Overall, the camp was bustling with people, but its structures were orderly and strategically arranged for defense and efficiency.

The Shadows ran to get in front of her, blocking her path. Runa tried to go around them, but they only stepped in front of her again.

With a huff Runa said, "I'm going to the village to check on the wounded."

"We can't let you do that, Lady Runa," Shadow One shook his head.

Well, that wasn't going to work for her. Runa crossed her arms and looked at the guards. "Bold of you to assume that was a suggestion."

The Shadows looked at each other, as if they were trying to read each other's minds. She had them on edge. Good. Runa put one hand on her hip.

"The only way you are going to stop me from going to the village is to drag me back to the camp. If you do, we will have to go before the Senshin and explain why you put your hands on me. Are you prepared to do that?"

The men went stiff. Runa took that as her cue. In their moment of hesitation, she slipped by the two men and continued walking towards the village.

She felt a tinge of guilt that her behavior would put them in a bad position. They would be punished because of her insubordination. But they were an extension of Keshin. Mindless bodies with pointy sticks. And she would not let Keshin dictate who she was allowed to heal and when.

The clanking noises told Runa that her Shadows were following her again. "Lady Runa, allow us to escort you."

Well, that was easier than she thought. Runa expected them to put up more of a fight.

Their journey out of the camp was made mostly in silence, Runa leading them through the warcamp to the newly formed path that would take them to the village of Sakanoue.

Once outside of the warcamp, she looked back over her shoulders to the two figures shadowing her steps. They hadn't hesitated when she gave them the choice. No questions. No conditions. For days now they've been following her like ghosts, always near, always silent, never offering their names. And she hadn't asked either, didn't want to know. They were tools of Keshin's control.

But now they were following her not because someone ordered them to—sort of. She was sure they were given the order to guard her and keep her safe. But they chose to follow her out of the village instead of forcing her back inside her tent. Runa thought that might mean something. And for that, they deserved names other than Shadow.

"What are your names?" Runa asked.

"Akio," Shadow One said, averting his gaze.

"Isaku," Shadow Two said with a smile.

"Thank you for not making this difficult."

"You didn't give us much of a choice," Akio grumbled.

He's right. But her conscience was still clear.

"If I may, honorable Iya—" Isaku started to say. Runa glared at him. "Lady Runa, why do you want to go to Sakanoue?"

"I've helped everyone in camp I can. After the recent battle, I'm sure there are villagers who could use my help. I'm also running low on medicine and other supplies."

"Like what?"

"White willow bark."

Akio and Isaku stared blankly.

"It reduces pain and swelling. I give it to people to chew on or make tea with it," Runa explained.

"Can't you resupply at camp?" Isaku asked.

"Are you suggesting I use what limited supplies the nurses have?"

"Why not ask the Senshin?" Akio asks.

That would require speaking to him, which Runa avoided whenever possible. The thought of asking Keshin anything turned Runa's stomach.

Though he'd probably have many words for her once he found out she left camp.

"I'm sure he's too busy for the frivolous needs of his subjects."

"You'd be surprised," Isaku said.

Runa pursed her lips again. "Why's that?"

"The Senshin is a great man."

A great man? She bit down on the thought like it tasted wrong. Keshin was irksome on the best days. He was prideful, arrogant, and too used to people bending to his will. Just because he didn't chain her to a wall or raise a hand to her didn't make him merciful or kind.

But she couldn't deny he had the respect of his men. Akio and Isaku wouldn't be vouching for him otherwise. Keshin's men followed him with the kind of loyalty you couldn't beat into someone. The whole "divinely blessed by the god of war" thing probably had something to do with it.

After all, even tyrants earned devotion. The line between fear and respect was razor thin.

Then Isaku had to go and say something she never expected. "He's in the village right now, helping the people rebuild. That's why we've stayed in this spot for so long."

"I thought he was waiting for peace talks with the other warlord?"

"Toraichi," Akio spat. "He called for a ceasefire and wanted a week to recover."

"Resupply is more like it," Isaku said.

"Either way, the Senshin agreed so we could help the people rebuild."

Runa pursed her lips. She found it hard to believe that a warlord would take the time to help the common people. She'd seen too much to believe in benevolent brutes. Warlords took and bled the people dry under the guise of protection.

But she didn't think that Isaku and Akio were lying to her either.

The contradiction sat heavy in her chest. It didn't add up.

"I doubt that's true," Runa said.

Isaku waved her off. "You'll see for yourself when we get to the village."

The rest of the journey Isaku and Akio exclaimed about Keshin, his bravery, his fairness, his resourcefulness. It made Runa want to vomit.

Keshin was nothing more than a blade, a brute blessed by Thar-aveld, the God of War, not reason. She didn't care how many lives he'd saved if he'd taken just as many. But something made Runa's stomach twist. They weren't fools. Isaku was sharp, and Akio could read her intentions like a scroll. So why did they see something where she couldn't? Or worse, why did part of her want to believe them?

As they reached the outskirts of the village, their path wound through rice paddies and vegetable gardens. A painter would love to capture such picturesque beauty if the town wasn't suffering wounds from the recent battle.

A mosaic of rustic cottages roofed with broken clay tiles or burned thatched straw huddled around a well-trodden central square. The pathways, little more than packed earth, twisted between the dwellings and led to a marketplace, shrine to Aylis, and finally, the bustling communal well.

As they walked through the town, Runa noticed how Keshin's soldiers were hard at work helping the denizens rebuild. Just because his soldiers were here though, didn't mean Keshin bothered to do the work himself.

"What now?" Isaku asked.

"I worked out of the shrine before I was captured," Runa explained. "I was going to go back there. People turn to the gods when they are in need of help."

The shrine was a modest wooden structure with a gradually curving roof flanked by stone lanterns leading up to the entrance where a young woman swept the front porch.

She looked up as the group approached. Her dark eyes went wide, her mouth hanging open.

"Lady Runa," she cried, running down the steps. Her dark hair, neatly pinned back, did not move, but her crimson-trimmed sleeves danced in the wind as she raced toward the trio.

She slid to a stop in front of Runa and dropped into a bow.

"Yumi," Runa said, with a smile as she returned the bow.

"We were so worried," Yumi's voice was breathless.

"I'm sorry to have worried you but I am okay," Runa said, pulling the sleeve of her robes down over her Unmei mark on her left hand so Yumi would not see it. At least not now.

Only then did Yumi seem to register that there were guards with Runa. She bowed again. "Forgive me, I am Yumi, the shrine maiden. All are welcome to the Sakanoue shrine."

Runa glanced sideways in time to catch it, Isaku's shoulders stiffening, his chin tilting just a touch too high. And then, unmistakably, the flush that bloomed up his neck and crept into his cheeks.

He was blushing.

Runa nearly choked on her own breath biting back a grin. Aylis, she hadn't seen that look since her novice days. Isaku was apparently rendered mute by the sight of Yumi.

Maybe the gods did have a sense of humor.

"We are here to escort Lady Runa and keep her safe," Akio bowed.

Yumi gave a smile that didn't quite lift the corners of her eyes. "Thank you for keeping her safe."

"It is our honor," Isaku seemed to find his voice. "As it is our honor to meet you."

Yumi smiled softly then turned to Runa. "Are you staying for a while?"

"I'd like to spend the day healing the people who need it most," Runa said.

"Praise Aylis," Yumi clasps her hands together. "There are a lot of injured people.

Yumi ushered them into the shrine. It was a serene atmosphere with polished wooden floors, minimalist decor, and a central altar where offerings were placed to all the gods.

"Please have a seat," Yumi said.

Runa lowered herself onto one of the cushions Yumi had placed on the floor, tucking her legs beneath her. "Isaku and Akio, please wait outside."

Both men hesitated at the threshold of the shrine.

"There's no threat to me inside this shrine."

Isaku's eyes narrowed, clearly unconvinced. "Akio will wait outside. I'll stay here."

It was a small compromise, one Runa would agree to. Akio bowed and stepped out of the shrine. Isaku took up a post in the front left corner so he could have a visual on both the door and Runa.

It didn't take long before an elderly woman arrived, her steps slow and cautious. Her arm was crudely bandaged and in a sling.

"Lady Runa," the woman's voice wavered. "I did not expect to see you again."

A common sentiment, Runa thought. "Please sit, let me help you."

Yumi helped the elderly woman settle on the mat across from her. With gentle hands, Runa handled the woman's arm, unwrapping it to show the blistered, angry red skin of a burn.

"Something fell on me while I was trying to get to safety," the elder explained.

"I'm going to heal this for you," Runa said.

With a breath, she centered her concentration and opened herself up to Aylis's divine energy. Runa's hands glowed white and the wound on the woman's arm began to close. The skin knitted itself back together until there was no trace of injury.

"There," Runa said when she finished.

The woman made her offering to the gods and left.

"Your eyes, Lady Runa, do they always turn turquoise?" Isaku asked.

Runa nodded. "Everytime I channel Aylis's power."

Soon the healer had a line of people waiting to see her. She laid her hands on patient after patient, each one with an injury worse than the one before. Burns of various degrees, broken bones, and lacerations. Come midday, Runa began to feel the first signs of exhaustion. Continuously channeling divine energy was taxing her body and mind. Her muscles strained and her movements slowed. It felt as if she had been running long distances. But, she could handle the fatigue. The real problem was the mental drain. She needed to remain concentrated on her healing. One wrong move meant she might mend something incorrectly, causing more harm than good.

Runa pressed on through the fuzzy vision, the burning sensation in her arms, and an empty stomach to keep restoring the injured.

As the sun reached its zenith, Runa was preparing to treat an elderly man lying before her when she heard a commotion in the crowd waiting outside the shrine. Despite the sound of knees dropping on stone, she focused on the task at hand.

Then she heard Akio speak outside the shrine, "Honorable Senshin."

Keshin had come for her. *That* took longer than expected.

Chapter 3

"Runa!" Keshin bellowed before flinging open the door.

As the sliding door slammed loudly against its frame, Yumi jumped and bowed deeply before the Senshin.

Runa did not move from her spot on the floor. Instead, she studied him intently. Despite her simmering loathing for the warlord, her eyes were drawn to his unarmored form. Keshin's white shirt, soaked with sweat, hinted at his muscular silhouette beneath.

What had he been doing? Isaku couldn't have been right about Keshin helping rebuild the town. He was probably training or doing something else with that sword of his.

Her gaze swept over his broad shoulders, to the angle of his jaw, which was covered in stubble, and to the strands of dark hair that escaped his topknot, falling to either side of his face.

Runa had only seen Keshin in his yoroi armor. Outside of it, the man was a piece of art.

Wait, what are you thinking? Runa chided herself. She refused to think of this brute as an attractive anything.

When Runa didn't respond to him, Keshin took a step towards her.

Her eyes flicked to Keshin staring at her as if she was the only thing in his field of view. He looked at her like a predator stalking its prey. She turned to face her patient, praying the rosy glow in her cheeks wouldn't betray her thoughts.

"Explain yourself," he demanded.

Ignoring the Senshin, Runa focused on the elderly man still lying on the ground. A burn encompassed his neck, shoulder, and the top of his chest. The elderly man had said a wooden beam set ablaze fell on him.

Hovering her hands over the man's injury, Runa inhaled deeply to steady her shaking hands. The goddess's energy poured out of her and into her patient as she channeled Aylis's divine light. She kneaded the air, fingers moving in wavelike motion as Runa passed her glowing hands over the singed skin, encouraging it to regenerate.

The man moaned in a combination of pain and relief as the skin knitted back together. Runa nodded toward Yumi who retrieved a piece of bark from Runa's bag and held it to the man's mouth.

"Chew on this, it will help." It was her last piece but he would need it. His healed skin would be tender and pink when she was done.

Keshin paced, his footsteps heavy on the wooden floors while she finished her ritual. Despite Keshin's palpable aggravation, the room was silent as she worked.

Runa breathed easy again once her task was complete. The man stood and rolled his shoulder, testing it. He bowed to Runa in thanks, then bowed to Keshin. He hesitated a brief second, then bowed to Runa again, before he left.

Once he was gone, Runa stood and stretched her arms out, rolling her head from side to side. Her body was stiff from the excessive use of her gifts and she felt unsteady on her feet. Despite putting on a strong face, she struggled to stay upright. Runa would only acknowledge Keshin when she was ready.

He stopped pacing to look at her, rooting himself like a mighty oak tree, eyes smoldering red with power. This was the first time he had seen her filled with Aylis's light, her normally golden eyes glowing turquoise.

His surprise brought her a hedonistic joy.

Shaking his head, Keshin took a deep breath, probably an attempt to regain his composure.

"You left camp," he finally stated

Runa stood before him, looking to her left and then to her right, checking her surroundings. "You're as observant as my Shadows. Maybe you should take notes from them and stick to the dark spaces where I can't see you. "

The muscle above Keshin's right eye twitched.

"Leave us," he commanded, his booming voice reverberated against the walls of the shrine.

Poor Yumi jumped to her feet and opened the door. Runa saw the crowd dispersing. Keshin's personal guard marched out of earshot and formed a perimeter.

Runa guessed this was as much privacy as they could have.

"You are using too much power," Keshin said.

"I'm healing the people your soldiers might have injured in the battle," Runa spat back at him.

"You don't understand. You are in danger—"

Runa cut him off. "I am always in danger!"

Her tone made Keshin pause. It was the first time she raised her voice to him. His stiff posture gave way and his eyebrows pulled together. It was as if he wanted her to continue or elaborate on what she meant.

Runa let out a small laugh and started pacing in the shrine. Where to even begin the explanation of her life: the past–what was it now–five years?

She looked to the altar that held symbols of all the gods. Reaching out, Runa's fingertips grazed over Aylis's symbol, a blooming lotus bursting with rays of light.

"I was sixteen when Aylis blessed me. I lived with my mother and my father in the far north of the Shirane province. I trained under the local temple, honed my skills, and helped the locals. Everything Aylis wanted from her blessed, I did, I was."

Pain gripped her heart and Runa took a breath, trying to push past to continue with the memory.

"Rumors of the Iyashite spread and the first warlord came before my seventeenth birthday. He and his men attacked the town, took my parents captive, and forced me to serve only him and his men."

Keshin shifted uncomfortably, but he remained silent.

"Another warlord came to claim me, attacking the first. We used it as a chance to escape. Except our path was blocked. My father died getting my mother and me out. I don't have anything to remember him by."

"What happened then?" Keshin asked.

"My mother and I fled south into Higashima province. Guess how many years before the next warlord came for me?"

"Runa—" Keshin said gently.

"Eight months. Guess how old I was when my mother and I separated?"

Keshin pursed his lips.

"I was eighteen years old. I left her in the middle of the night so she could have a chance at a normal life." Runa's voice cracked.

It had been three years since she'd seen her mother. Runa had no idea if she was even alive.

"I kept moving south. Through Nakagawa Province where a local lord tried to welcome me into his service by bribing me with wealth, finery, jewelry, and finally, with force. A shrine maiden helped me escape that time. Took my place while I was sleeping."

Maybe that was why she felt so connected to Yumi.

"I learned to keep a low profile, sought refuge at local temples instead of inns where gossip spreads. But even now, here I am in Tensho Providence with two more warlords fighting."

"Finding you was not what brought me here," Keshin said.

"I find that hard to believe." Runa didn't entirely trust Keshin's word.

"Of course stories of the Iyashite being nearby reached my ears."

"You knew who I was," Runa accused.

"Because of your aura," Keshin explained.

Well, that would make sense. She knew who he was because of his aura.

"If you did not come for me, then why are you here? Why start a fight in this village?"

"You do not care why I am here. You have made your disdain for me and my men clear."

Runa had to stop herself from physically recoiling.

"I care that you treat me like I'm a spoil of this war."

"If you felt that way you should have come to me."

"Why? So you can post more guards around me?" Runa clenched her jaw, biting back the retort that burned on her tongue.

Isaku had said the same thing. But they'll never understand. How easy it was for men like Keshin to throw around words like trust. As if it were that simple. She learned long ago that needing someone came with a cost. Keshin might be divinely bound to her, but that didn't make him safe. And that definitely didn't mean she could surrender the armor she'd forged from solitude and suspicion.

"We are bonded," he said like Runa could forget. "I must keep you safe."

"You can't use the excuse of keeping me safe to prevent me from fulfilling my divinely ordained purpose!" she cut him off, her power burning behind her eyes. She was done listening to whatever lecture he was about to give.

A moment of silence passed between them.

"You are not content healing the wounded in camp?"

"Why do you think I am here?"

Now Runa felt like they were talking in circles. She needed to get back to healing people. She moved toward the door of the shrine to poke her head out, looking for anyone who might have lingered. There were only soldiers.

"What are you looking for?" Keshin asked.

"My next patient, but you scared them all away."

"No. We are returning to camp. You can return tomorrow with a proper escort."

"I can keep going now," Runa said.

It was a half-truth. She was honestly surprised she healed as many people as she had. It was a new record for her. Aylis should be proud.

"You can barely stand. We are returning to camp."

"No thank you," Runa said, reveling in the shade of mahogany Keshin's face turned. He paused, assessing her with his mahogany eyes. With blindingly fast footwork, Keshin closed the distance between them and hoisted Runa over his shoulder. He carried her out of the shrine and into the town. His retinue scrambled to follow their general.

Once she got over her shock, Runa pounded on Keshin's back. "Put me down!"

Goddess, this was embarrassing. Being hauled around like a petulant child.

Keshin, in fact, did not put her down, no matter how many times Runa struck him. But her fatigue and exhaustion from the day caught up with her, and by the time they reached the edge of town, Runa couldn't fight anymore.

Resigned to her fate, Runa slumped against his back.

"I hate you."

"I'm aware," Keshin said. "You are also exhausted."

"I am not."

"Do not lie to me," Keshin growled. "We are bonded, I can feel how tired you are."

What did he mean by that? It was then that Runa noticed the quake in the arm pinning her to Keshin's shoulder.

"You could feel me healing?" she asked.

"I felt you pull energy from me when I assume you exhausted your own reserves."

If she was pulling energy from Keshin, that would explain why she was able to heal for longer today than she normally could.

But the knowledge that she and Keshin's powers were bonded deeper than just these marks on their wrist terrified her. What did that mean when he went into battle? If she could siphon endurance from him, could he do the same from her?

"Can you walk on your own now?"

"Yes," Runa said weakly with dozens of different possibilities running through her mind.

Keshin gently lowered her from his shoulder, his hands lingering on her waist as he ensured she was steady on her feet. Unconsciously, Runa's hands fell to his forearms.

"What does this mean?" Runa asked, looking up into Keshin's eyes.

"I do not know. I suspect Tharaveld is as forthcoming as Aylis with their intentions."

Runa laughed.

"We will explore this after you are rested. Come, we are returning to camp."

Only then did Runa notice the herd of horses gathered at the edge of town. Runa may have walked here, but she doubted she was walking back.

An attendant untethered a beautiful black horse with his mane cut short. The younger man brought the stallion over to Keshin.

Without a word, Keshin stepped forward and lifted Runa by the waist. Her breath caught, not because he was rough, but because he wasn't. His grip was sure, careful, as if he knew exactly how much strength to use. Her feet left the ground and a heartbeat later she was settled in the saddle.

Runa barely had time to shift before Keshin mounted behind her in one fluid motion. His broad chest against her back, his thighs bracketing hers. He was so warm, even through the fabric of her robes. Aylis help her, his arms came around her waist to grasp the reins.

He didn't touch her more than necessary. But his nearness was inescapable.

Keshin spurred the horse forward, hooves thudding softly against packed earth as they rode toward the camp.

She stared straight ahead, her hands fisting the saddle, the wind tugging at her sleeves. The horse's gait pressed her back against Keshin and made her achingly aware of just how solid he was, how quiet, how calm.

For once they weren't fighting.

Runa was the one to break the silence. "You never answered my question, what are you doing here?"

Keshin was quiet to the point that Runa wondered if he would answer at all.

"Toraichi is the chief advisor for his son, a warlord who was married into the ruling family of the Kuwana Providence."

His voice seemed to consume her. The timbre vibrated at her back while his mouth was next to her ear. Runa focused on a point in front of them, focused on keeping her breathing steady. She would not let herself be affected by this man.

"He rules on behalf of his infant son and takes what lands he believes are his," Keshin continued.

Toraichi was the acting ruler of the Kuwana Province who shared a Northwest border with Keshin's lands, the Tensho Province.

"Your lands."

"I'm defending my people, trying to bring peace to the land, not perpetuate war."

"What else am I supposed to think?" Runa cried in defense.

Running from men like him was all she'd ever known.

"That your life isn't any more or less important than others."

"I do not think that," Runa protested.

"Your actions say otherwise. You neglect to even ask me when you need something."

She might not agree with the other things, but he had a point.

Runa hadn't asked for help, hadn't even considered asking for it. She just assumed he wouldn't give it, or that if he did, the price would be something she wasn't willing to pay. That was a lesson the world had taught her. Power always came with a cost, and kindness always came with a catch.

By the time they reached Keshin's camp, the sun was descending towards the horizon. As they approached Runa's tent she knew that if she wanted to ask, now would be the time. What if he was telling the truth? What if, for once, she didn't have to carry everything alone?

After turning their conversation over in her head, she was starting to believe that Keshin wasn't asking for blind faith. He was offering space where he might support her.

Before she entered her tent, Runa straightened her spine and kept her voice even as she said the words that tasted like fear and freedom. "I need medicine for the town. White willow bark among other things."

Keshin nodded, then pointed toward her tent. "Rest."

"Will my request be honored?"

Keshin simply nodded his head once, then ordered two guards to be stationed outside her tent. He was turning to leave when she stopped him.

"Please do not punish Isaku and Akio for escorting me to town."

Keshin's head snapped to look at her, his gaze firm. "Are you trying to tell me what to do with my men?"

"I'm saying that I played a part in coercing them to do what I wanted."

He seemed to mull over the information before he said, "I will consider it."

Then he walked off.

Inside her tent were her two attendants who had buckets of water with steam rising from them. Runa had to admit it was a welcomed sight. Runa disrobed and let the women rub sponges with water and soap over her body. The warmth seeped into her aching muscles, releasing the tension.

Her heart still remained heavy; her mind drifting back to the harsh words Keshin used.

Aylis had to know she didn't think of herself as better than any soldier who had given their life right? But how else was she supposed to know? All the warlords she met before were the same. Yet Keshin seemed to directly contradict that belief. She didn't know much about Toraichi, this other warlord Keshin was fighting, but she was sure the Senshin and his men were the only ones helping rebuild the village.

Shame stuck to her like molasses that wouldn't wipe away with each swipe of the sponges. Guilt twisted in her stomach as the women dried her, dressed her, and left her to sleep that night.

She had to be better—do better.

The next morning Runa awoke to a bundle of white willow bark beside her bed. A faint smile crossed her lips. One battle down, but it felt like she and Keshin had an entire war to go.

Chapter 4

For the next three days, Keshin personally escorted her into Sakanoue. At first, he expected her to ride with him again—an idea she swiftly shot down.

"One shared ride was enough don't you think?"

Keshin nodded and ordered another horse to be saddled. A dapple grey mare was brought forward, slightly smaller than Keshin's warhorse. One more Runa's size.

She took a moment to pack the saddlebags with supplies before she attempted to mount. It took a moment for Runa to find her balance enough to swing up in the saddle, but once she had her seat moving with the steed came naturally.

Keshin gave her a curt nod and guided his horse in the direction of the village.

Thankfully, their ride was silent. Mostly because Keshin took up a position ahead of her. Though she could still yell to him if she felt inclined.

Their traveling party was large. Not only did Isaku and Akio ride with her, but there were six other soldiers assigned to her, all reporting to Isaku. Runa's very on squad.

In addition, Keshin's second in command, Hoshi, and his other officers, many whom she recognized from that first night in Keshin's tent, were there.

Today, Keshin was talking with Toraichi, the opposing army's leader. Hopefully, the two lords could come to an agreement about territory without further need for violence.

To Runa, it seemed like a whole lot of posturing. Still, Runa was hopeful.

"Have you met this Toraichi before?"

"Never seen him," Isaku said. "I heard he looks like a salamander."

Runa stifled a laugh imagining this elderly wrinkled man sitting across from Keshin who had both more power and a better jawline.

It's unfair, really—that someone so insufferable could also be well... *that*.

Runa shook her head. She couldn't be thinking about Keshin that way.

As they rode into the village she could see repaired roofs, rebuilt walls, and repaved roads. The people too looked happier. All signs that their work was coming to an end.

Normally she would move onto the next town, but she wasn't sure how that would work now that she was bonded to Keshin. He had an entire province to rule and she'd been nomadic these past few years.

While he'd been accommodating to her needs, asking Keshin to let her leave was an entirely different request.

Would he even let her?

She'd broach the subject with him later.

They arrived outside the tents where the peace talks were to occur, and their party slowed down. Keshin swung off his horse and approached the left side of Runa's horse.

"Remember—"

"Don't waste your breath, I'll be fine."

Aylis, she pulled from his power one time and he reminded her everyday. How was she supposed to know that was possible? They still hadn't figured out how.

Keshin pursed his lips, but didn't fight her. "Send someone if you need anything."

She doubted she'd need anything. Not out of her refusal, but because Keshin had given her everything she asked for, and more.

Now, picking her up and tossing her over his shoulder against her will, that one she was still working on.

Briefly, Runa wondered if she had judged him too harshly?

Probably not.

Runa dismounted, handed the reins of her horse to someone, and walked the rest of the way with her squad of soldiers to the shrine.

Yumi greeted them. Isaku ordered the others to make a perimeter while he managed the line outside the shrine. Akio would be in the shrine with them.

Yumi seemed to deflate at that.

Runa took her spot on the floor cushion and waited. As before, it did not take long for her patients to line up.

"Are you ready for the next patient?" Yumi said, a little too eager to go open the door.

Runa almost commented on the color in the shrine maiden's cheeks as she opened the door to speak to Isaku. It seems the soldier's infatuation with the shrine maiden was reciprocated.

A sad smile crossed her face. Runa would never get to know that feeling. Any chance she had at love vanished when Aylis decided she should be bonded to Keshin. On the best of days, they were merely civil towards each other, but most days they treated each other with indifference. She secretly coveted Yumi's organic connection with Isaku.

Sadly for them, if the peace talks went well today, both armies would be leaving.

"This way, sir." Yumi held the door as a weathered, battled-worn, middle-aged man entered the shrine.

Runa did a quick visual assessment, looking for blood, cuts, and bruises. There were none. The man's build was solid for his age. Runa might have mistaken him for a soldier if not for the limp to his left leg and his lack of colors declaring him as serving under either warlord.

She wasn't surprised at his seemingly minor malady. Having healed the most life-threatening injuries on her first day, most of the patients she saw now either had minor wounds or a lingering illness from before the attack. Spending the energy to fix his knee might seem to the unblessed like a waste of her talents. But if Runa could improve the quality of the man's life while she was in the village, she would.

"Honorable Iyashite," her new patient stopped before her and bowed.

Runa gave a small nod of her head, acknowledging the man's respect, then gestured for him to take a seat on the mat before her. "Please call me Runa, and tell me how I can help you."

A few seconds passed and the man did not sit or kneel. Runa wondered if his knee bothered him too much.

"But you are the Iyashite?" the man asked.

Runa's brows pulled together. "Yes, but I insist you call me Runa, or Lady Runa if you must."

The man nodded and laid down on the mat before her. Taking a deep breath, Runa reached into the well of power Aylis granted her, drawing it up and into her body to channel her divine gift. She held her hands out over the man's body, letting the energy flow from her into him. She started at his chest, checking his heart and other major organs. Nothing wrong there. Her hands traveled over his torso to his knee. Nothing wrong there either.

Her eyebrows furrowed. When he walked in, the man had a visible limp. That could be caused by some sort of knee, or even hip injury. But she couldn't find anything wrong. Aylis's power had never led her wrong. Logically, there was only one option.

Runa withdrew her power from the man's body. "You are healthy as an ox, sir."

"So, there's nothing you can do for me?" The man asked, sitting up.

"My apologies but no, there's nothing more I can do."

"I just wanted to see if you were real," the man said as he stood, dusted off his clothes, and walked back towards the shrine door. This time, without the limp.

Mouth open, Runa looked to Yumi who had a similar baffled expression on her face. She was no stranger to people wondering if she was truly Alyis's blessed. But usually those individuals were in poor health and had little hope otherwise. This man came in here, knowing he was healthy, just to see if she was real. What a waste of her time.

And that got under her skin more than Keshin could.

Before she knew what was happening, Runa was on her feet, following the man out the door and down the steps. The man was regrouping with two others who stood at the base of the temple. They turned and headed into town.

"Lady Runa," Yumi asked, slightly out of breath from hurrying after her.

"Do you know that man?" Runa asked.

Yumi shook her head. "No, my lady."

Something was off here, Runa knew it in the way her stomach turned. In the way the other villagers gave him a wide berth and whispered to each other.

"Lady Runa," Akio appeared next to them. "Is something wrong?"

"I'm going to follow that man," Runa said. "Akio come with me. Yumi, tell Isaku and treat who you can."

And Runa was on the move again, doing her best to track the man through the village. If he heard her, he gave no indication.

"He's headed in the direction of the summit tent," Akio whispered to her as best they could as he weaved through people and buildings.

"Why is he going there?" Runa wondered to herself.

Sure enough, when they reached the outskirts of the village, the interloper and his friends headed straight for the central tent with Keshin and Toraichi's banners decorating the outside.

Some of Keshin's soldiers shifted nervously as if they wanted to leave. However, the men dressed in Toraichi's colors bowed to the man, and stepped aside, allowing him entrance into the tent.

Biting her lip, Runa tried to make sense of the man's actions. He faked an ailment to see her and then went straight to the summit tent. Toraichi's men recognized him, so maybe he was an advisor of some sort?

"I don't think we can follow him," Akio said.

Maybe, *he* couldn't.

Runa straightened her robes, held her head high, and approached the tent. This time, as she approached, Toraichi's soldiers went to stop her, probably with some no women allowed nonsense.

"Lady Runa," one of Keshin's soldiers, bowed.

"Open the tent," she ordered.

Runa had never truly ordered Keshin's men. She assumed she didn't have that authority. But now she had to try.

With a nod, the soldier pulled back the tent's fabric door and Runa stepped through.

Inside, the space was lit by soft daylight filtering through thin panels, casting a diffused golden glow over everything.

Thick woven rugs lined the floor, muting footsteps and separating the room from the cold, packed dirt below. In the center stood a low lacquered table, its dark surface gleaming, flanked by neatly arranged floor cushions. Braziers burned in corners, the scent of sandalwood and cypress threading through the air.

Keshin was standing on the right side of the table, flanked by Hoshi and another advisor, also standing. She could feel Keshin aura swirling around him, angry, lashing out at the man, still seated across the table.

Toraichi.

Isaku was right, he looked like a salamander: leathery, scaly skin, thinning hair, mouth pulled into a wide grin with narrow eyes.

"What are you playing at?" Hoshi demanded.

"I could ask you the same thing," Toriachi nodded toward Runa.

Keshin's gaze flicked to hers. Runa caught him doing a quick scan of her body in the same way she examined a patient for injuries.

When their eyes connected again, something unspoken passed between them.

You are unharmed?

Runa gave a barely perceptible nod, then flicked her eyes towards the pretender.

I don't like him.

"Lady Runa is my guest," Keshin chose his words carefully.

"She's more than that," the man from the temple said. Then, approaching the seated Toraichi he said, "Out of my chair boy."

This man used the word "boy" to belittle a fully grown man. That's the type of arrogance she'd expect from an entitled commander. And the way everyone bowed to him suggested he was high-ranking.

The fake warlord stood, "The seat is yours, Lord Toraichi."

Then the true Lord Toraichi took his place at the table as the scaly man moved to the seat to his lord's right.

It was a ruse. Runa's interloper had been the real Toraichi. The scaly man was only a stand in.

"You should take a seat, Lord Senshin," The real Toraichi said, a smirk on his lips.

"You will explain this deception or these talks are over," Keshin demanded.

Even with his back to her, Runa could feel the waves of power rolling off of Keshin like smoke rising from a stoked fire. Despite the smoldering coals of his anger, Keshin kept his composure.

"We were negotiating in good faith," Hoshi said.

"I needed a better understanding of what you had to offer me before making my demands." The real Toraichi looked pointedly at Runa.

The healer pursed her lips. He just insulted her, abasing her as an asset. A thing, a resource, a spoil of war that Keshin had claimed. Bile burned the back of her throat as her skin heated. She felt her power course through her, eyes changing color.

"I had heard you captured the Iyashite and brought her to your...personal quarters," Toraichi said.

Rage turned to embarrassment as a blush rose on her cheeks. The fucker's assumptions weren't inaccurate. The soldiers who found her brought her to Keshin's tent that first night. But nothing Toraichi implied had happened.

"Runa is not my possession," Keshin stated.

She couldn't see his face, but through their bond, Runa felt Keshin's power flare. Imagining his mahogany eyes bleeding red, Runa decided it was best to remain silent—for once.

"Sure she is," Toraichi said dismissively. "She's a woman, and now your Iyashite."

"One cannot own that which is of the divine. You will address her with the respect afforded to her by her station."

Toraichi sneered, "I will do as I please."

Keshin was going to respond but Toraichi spoke first, "Let us make this simple. I want your Iyashite. Give her to me and I'll take my armies and leave, surrendering these lands to you."

Chapter 5

A ll the color drained from Runa's face. The words hit her like a slap, but she didn't flinch. She learned long ago how to wear stillness like armor.

It wasn't new, men trying to wrap her worth up in titles and power, never once asking what she wanted. They saw her blessing, not her. She was seen as a tool, a thing to be used. A means to meet someone else's end.

Toraichi hadn't directed his offer to her, as if she wasn't standing right there in the room with them. He only saw her as part of the negotiations, something to be bartered in exchange for peace.

That told her everything she needed to know about this man. It made her stomach twist in knots.

Still, Runa could understand if Keshin was considering it. With one affirmation, he could ensure the lives of his men, the villagers, and the immediate retreat of the opposing force in exchange for her.

Keshin stood still, towering over the older man. Runa did not miss the way Hoshi had shifted, putting himself between her and Toraichi's men. Not blocking her, but in a position to defend her if need be.

"You cannot give me lands that are not yours to give," Keshin said, his voice low and tinged with warning.

"Details," Toraichi said with a wave of his hand. "The fighting between our camps can cease if you simply hand her over to me."

Runa clenched her fists inside the sleeves of her robes. The anger built inside her as she fought to keep her composure. Nothing would bring her greater pleasure than telling this pig to shove these terms up his ass. While Keshin tolerated her sass, she doubted Toraichi enjoyed women talking out of turn–if at all.

"You so freely disrespect one blessed by the gods."

"I'm sure you will forgive me when I hand over my lands to you."

"I do not refer to myself."

"She is a woman."

"Lady Runa is *the* Iyashite, blessed by the goddess, Aylis."

"What is your answer, *Lord Senshin*?" Toraichi all but spat the title out.

Keshin paused, turning his head to look at her. "The choice is Runa's."

She stared at him, hardly believing what she'd heard. Keshin was giving her a choice. Not a command. Not an order wrapped in politeness. Not a demand masquerading as duty.

A real choice.

To stay by his side, or to go with Toraichi.

He was telling her that he would defend her, he would stand against this man for her.

But Runa almost didn't want this choice. Not like this. She'd spent her life running from cages, even gilded ones. She fought to hold onto what little freedom she had. And here stood one man, carved from war and quiet patience, asking her to choose.

Except choosing him didn't feel like a cage.

That was terrifying.

It felt like he was creating a space for her. Somewhere she could step into if she wanted. Or walk away from.

No one had ever offered her that.

Not once.

She doubted Toraichi would ever do the same. She'd be a trophy, a tool, a concubine—or worse.

Her pulse thudded in her throat. Her voice felt too far away. And still, the question hung between them, waiting.

The choice was simple.

Runa raised her left hand, letting her sleeve fall, revealing her Unmei mark. She spoke to the room, but only looked at Keshin. "We are bonded."

Runa swore she felt a surge of strength across the bond.

Toraichi's smugness faded and his mouth pulled into a thin line as he took in this new information.

Keshin revealed his matching Unmei mark, holding his hand out to Runa. She acquiesced, placing her hand atop his. Calloused fingers tentatively wrapped around hers, a thumb swiping against the skin there.

Standing, Toraichi straightens his robes. "Then we have nothing else to discuss."

He swiftly leaves the tent, followed by his advisors, general, and attendants.

Silence overtook the tent as the weight of the decisions settled around them. Until one foolishly brave soul stepped forward. "My lord, is she worth it?"

Was she worth not handing over to Toraichi to broker a peace deal? Runa could not help but think the same thing. Staying with Keshin meant she could doom dozens, even hundreds of men, all because she was selfish. All because she wanted freedom.

But she had chosen herself, not because the gods demanded it, not because Keshin had pressed her, but because she wanted to.

Was her freedom worth the bloodshed? Had she made the right choice?

Her breath caught as she waited for Keshin to respond with some cold indifference. Maybe a shrug. Mostly silence.

But what followed was not silence—it was heat.

A pulse of power rolled through the tent like thunder beneath the skin. The floor trembled. The air thickened, heavy with the scent of smoke and steel. From beside her, Keshin took a step forward.

When Runa glanced at him, his eyes were blazing crimson red. Every muscle in his body was coiled, jaw tight, shoulders squared, barely restrained.

"Watch your tongue," he said, voice low and simmering. "You forget in whose presence you stand."

The man fell to the ground with a thud and he pressed his hands and forehead to the dirt, refusing to meet their eyes. "My apologies to my lord."

"I would have your life for this disrespect," Keshin said, drawing his katana and holding it to the man's neck. "But forgiveness is not mine to grant."

Runa felt everyone's attention shift to her.

She'd expected Keshin to deliver punishment himself, to snap a command—or neck—and be done with it.

But instead, he waited. No spectacle. No whispered suggestion. Just silence and a man on his knees waiting for her judgement.

Runa met Keshin's eyes, her question lingered between them. *Are you sure?*

"A disrespect to you is a disrespect to me," Keshin answered.

She returned to her attention to the offender. She could order Keshin to take his life, like he offered. But she didn't need this man's blood. She needed him to understand.

"You will clean the latrines for the next month," Runa ordered, giving him a consequence, not cruelty.

"See that it's done," Keshin addressed somebody, but Runa didn't see who because Keshin's hand found her lower back as he guided her toward the tent entrance.

He might as well be burning a hole through the back of her robes.

"Are you finished with your healing for the day?" His words were terse and she understood. Today did not go as planned—for either of them.

If she was being honest, after everything that happened inside that tent, healing was the last thing on Runa's mind.

"Yes."

"Akio," Keshin called to his retinue. "Return to the shrine and inform the others that Lady Runa will not be returning for the day."

"Yes sir," Akio bowed, and then walked off.

"Keshin—"

"Not here," he said curtly.

Not another word passed between them as Keshin approached their horses. One of the men moved to help Runa mount a steed, but Keshin put his arm out, stopping the man.

Again, Keshin lifted her atop the steed. This time, he did not follow. Instead, he approached his black stallion and mounted it. He looked at her, then spurred his steed in the direction of the camp. Runa squeezed her heels into her mare's side to spur the horse, trying to catch up to him.

Together they rode along the trodden path between Keshin's camp and Sakanoue.

Runa could feel the anger, the fury rolling off of him in waves. For the first time since they met, she felt like she was seeing Keshin wrestle with his temper. She noted how his men gave him plenty of space and took their time following him back to the camp. But she wasn't afraid of Keshin's moods.

She was his equal. And right now, it was just the two of them and the gods looking down upon them.

"I am sorry things didn't work out with Toraichi."

Keshin gripped the reins tighter. "You should sleep in my tent tonight."

That was a big fat no. "Placing my tent next to yours isn't good enough?"

"After that disaster? I only trust myself to keep you safe."

Runa rolled her eyes. They were back to this. "What do you think could happen to me when I'm sleeping one tent away from you?"

"It's obvious Toraichi wants you. If he was willing to give up everything just to have you, what lengths do you think he will go to when he's denied?"

"It's not like you can stay awake all night just to guard me."

"It wouldn't be the first time."

Wait, was he saying that it wasn't his first time staying up all night or wasn't his first time protecting a woman? And why did the second option bother her?

"Why should I sleep in your tent tonight?"

"Toraichi is a man who is used to getting what he wants."

Since Keshin brought him up, Runa felt comfortable enough asking, "I thought my life was not any more or less important than that of your men."

"But it is still your own," Keshin said. "Food, land, weapons, they are things. Women are not objects to be traded. Your life is your own."

"I should ... I need ... thank you," Runa tried to find the words. "You gave me the choice. I know what it cost you."

"Gratitude is a new look for you," Keshin responded.

She immediately regretted saying anything. Yet, his comment meant a return to their usual discourse. A welcome change to the serious warlord he had to be in those situations.

"Are you shocked?"

"That you're using a modicum of common decency with me?" Keshin's tone was harsh, but Runa caught a tinge of humor within it. "Astounded."

"It was incredibly difficult," Runa quipped back.

Keshin grunted.

Silence drifted between them like mist on a pond. But the longer the silence went on, the more his anger seemed to recede like the tide.

This time, he broke the silence. "I meant it."

"What?"

"You belong to no one Runa."

"Even you?"

"You are my bonded, my equal, not my possession."

"I can't hate you the way I want if you say things like that."

Keshin finally turned to look at her, his sharpness dulled. He looked more like a man again, not a warlord, not a weapon.

"You don't have to hate me Runa."

Runa's breath caught, not from the words, but from the way he said them.

"You make it sound so simple."

"It is that simple."

Another silence, but this one didn't weigh. It stretched.

"If the gods hadn't marked us, would you still have stayed?" Keshin asked.

Runa didn't answer right away, her focus shifting to each step her horse made.

"I don't know," she finally whispered. "Would you have honestly let me leave?"

Keshin was quiet for a while. But then he said, "If that's what you wished."

"You'd let me go?"

"With protection, yes."

Runa sat, stewing with that information. Something about that statement made Runa's heart sink. She didn't understand why the thought of Keshin letting her go made her feel ... unsettled.

Keshin looked at her like she just asked the most ridiculous question.

Then he leaned in closer to her. "I'm glad you chose what the gods want for us."

There was an undertone of something more in his words. Yes, the gods brought them together, but knowing Keshin wanted her there for himself and not solely because of the will of the gods meant more to her.

Turning her face slightly, Runa glanced at Keshin. "I haven't made my choice yet."

Keshin smirked, "You're still here,"

They rode in silence after that, but it felt different. The wind brushed against her cheeks, and she was acutely aware of the space between them. And how small it had become.

As they neared the edge of the camp, Runa spoke again, her voice barely louder than the breeze.

"I don't hate you."

She didn't turn to see his reaction. She didn't need to.

"I know."

And for now, that was enough.

Chapter 6

That evening, night blanketed the land in its gentle embrace, but sleep still evaded Runa. She lay awake in her own bed, in her separate tent, the covers pulled around her, staring up at—well, nothing. Her mind was elsewhere.

Specifically, back on a horse with Keshin as they rode toward the camp.

Not only had Keshin given her the choice to stay with him throughout the peace talks, but he said he would let her go. She wasn't the captive she thought.

While faint, she still felt the warmth of his hand on her abdomen. The sensation stirred something inside her, making her feel ... odd, like heat pooled within her abdomen.

Runa rolled over to her side, her back to the door. The camp was a strange juxtaposition of lively and quiet. Quiet as the stillness of the night lulled many of the soldiers to sleep. But lively because Runa swore she could hear every small sound. There was the shuffle of footsteps, distant moaning, and—was that some guy urinating?

Gross.

But she had chosen to stay in this camp. Stay with him. Keshin had given her that freedom, and still she chose *him*. Not because she trusted him, not yet, not fully, but because something in her heart whispered that he might be more than the war-forged shell he showed the world. The thought chipped at her resolve.

Maybe, just maybe, he wasn't the monster she'd made him out to be.

The gods had tied her fate to his, that much was undeniable. But for the first time since the mark appeared on her hand, Runa wondered if fate was more than a chain. Perhaps it was a path. One she didn't choose, but one she could walk on her own terms.

That idea scared her.

It was easier to hate Keshin when he fit neatly into the role of captor, brute, but now ... now he was something else. A man who watched her with quiet patience. A man who bled for others. A man who let her decide.

Her fingers brushed over the red mark on her left hand, the red thread that curled like a brand around her skin. A strange kind of comfort, like a hearth lit in the dark. And maybe, though she was loath to admit it, the mark had started to feel less like a curse and more like a call. To belong. To matter to someone.

The ache in her chest wasn't fear. It was something far more dangerous.

Hope.

With a deep exhale Runa sat up in her bed, her gaze drifting between the objects she'd acquired during her stay. Since her time in the camp, Keshin had gifted her with more possessions than she had in her entire life. Sure, she had small mementos from her mother and father. But she couldn't remember ever having an ornate chest and weeks worth of clothing, fully stocked baskets of medicinal herbs, and the latest gift—a writing desk with parchment.

Rising from her bed, Runa crossed the tent to sit at her desk. She wrote instructions on a scroll to Yumi, describing signs of sickness and disease, as well as methods for treatment. The maiden would be able to apply the knowledge in her spiritual duties once Runa departed.

She would miss Yumi. Leaving behind this valuable information that would help generations to come was another way she honored Aylis's teachings, but to leave it for Yumi was a pleasure. Without Keshin's generosity, none of this would be possible.

Unrolling the scroll, Runa picked up her brush to begin again when she heard a choking and sputtering coming from one of the Shadows posted to guard her tent.

Akio couldn't be sick, could he? He looked fine earlier this morning. The last thing this camp needed was some illness to take soldiers out of commission, or worse, claim some of their lives.

Better stop this now before it got out of hand.

As Runa went to stand, she felt a wave of fatigue roll through her body. Her legs gave out and she tumbled to the ground. It felt as if someone was siphoning her power—impossible. The sensation was over as quickly as it had come upon her. Climbing to her feet, Runa noticed her left arm tingled and her skin was particularly warm.

What was that? Then she recalled how Keshin mentioned he could feel her drawing from his power the day she over-exerted herself. This could be the same. Except, why was Keshin overextending his power? There was no battle today and Keshin wasn't injured.

Yet, Runa couldn't shake the feeling that something wasn't right. As she was rushing to the front of her tent, Runa felt another wave of her divine power being ripped from her. Her vision blurred, and it took all her strength to stay upright.

There was no good reason why Keshin would tap into her power twice. She needed to find out what was going on.

The camp was quiet. Why had no one been alerted? She did not hear the heavy footsteps of soldiers rushing to their lord's aid.

"Guards!" she called.

The one time she called for her attendants and nobody responded.

Cautiously, Runa crept to the entrance. Looking down, she noticed a deep crimson stain absorbed into the fabric of the tent. Her hands flew to cover her mouth. She would know that color anywhere. Reaching for the hem of the door flap, Runa slowly pulled back the fabric to reveal Akio and the other guard prone on the ground, blood pooling around them. Tears pooled behind Runa's eyes as she choked back a sob.

Runa could only think of one type of person who would do this. Toraichi must have sent shinobi, elite assassins, into their camp.

But if they attacked her guards, why didn't they kidnap her?

Her eyes locked onto Keshin's tent, his personal guard lying in pools of their own blood, while two shadows danced among the glow of the fire inside his tent. They were trying to kill him before they took her, hoping she was fast asleep in her tent and they didn't have to worry about her raising the alarm.

She had to help him somehow. What could she do though? She wasn't a fighter.

Leaving Keshin to die didn't feel right. She didn't know how that would affect their bond either. Would she die if he did?

Swallowing her fear, Runa picked up Akio's tanto, a short blade. Unsheathing the weapon, she crouched down and inched her way toward Keshin's tent. With each step, she did her best not to make any sound, yet she felt the tension mounting in her body. Her hands clenched the hilt of the brandished weapon.

Reaching Keshin's tent, she paused to listen. She heard quick movements and the swoosh of steel cutting the air. Runa could only hope she didn't alert the intruder to her presence as well.

With shaking hands, she pulled back Keshin's door flap. Runa's eyes went wide with horror as the shinobi, dressed in dark clothes with his face concealed, had a kunai-like knife buried in the side of Keshin's neck.

It was a fatal wound, but maybe, if she could get to Keshin fast enough and pray for Aylis's mercy, Runa might be able to save him.

Keshin's hands gripped the shinobi's wrists and forced the other man to withdraw the kunai. Blood sprayed from the wound.

Runa channeled all her fear, her adrenaline, and her anger as she readied the tanto and rushed towards the shinobi.

Before the shinobi could register the new piece on this board, Runa separated his head from his body with a single horizontal slice.

As the severed head fell to the floor, blood spurted from the wound, soaking Runa, Keshin, and the interior of the tent. The metallic taste of blood filled her mouth.

Dropping the tanto, Runa rushed to Keshin's side, eyes glowing as she called upon Aylis' divine power.

"It's okay, I have you," she said.

As she brought her hands to his neck, she tried to find that calm center of Aylis's power within her. It was as if the well of healing energy had run dry.

She could not lose Keshin. Not this way. He was strong, blessed by Tharaveld, he couldn't be taken down in such a dishonorable way. Runa would save him. She had to.

She used the fabric of her robes to smear the blood away from his neck wound to get a better visual, only to find the wound had already healed. How did that happen? Her hands flit over his body, looking for other injuries. There were two other freshly healed wounds on Keshin's bloodstained chest. Those had to be wounds he healed when he siphoned her power. How much pain had he endured?

"Keshin," Runa whispered. "Look at me."

Opening his eyes, Runa took in the turquoise glow of Keshin's stare.

He reached up to cup her face, concern written on his features. "Why are your eyes red?"

Chapter 7

K eshin's eyes were glowing turquoise. He was channeling Aylis's power.

But he said her eyes were glowing red.

Runa's gaze drifted to the decapitated head lying next to her on the ground. There was no way she could have done that on her own with no formal training. She must have channeled Tharaveld's power to have the strength to do that.

Her body began to violently shake, her breaths unsteady and shallow coming in quick succession.

She killed a man. Her hands were meant for healing, not for this. She did it to save Keshin, but she still took a life. Precious life which Aylis considered sacred.

Not that she was a stranger to death. There were patients she could not save, but his death was a direct result of her actions.

Only then did she notice the bodies around her. Keshin must have felled two shinobi before this third stuck their kunai into the soft flesh of his neck.

On hands and knees, Runa emptied the contents of her stomach. Her lungs began to scream for air, unsatisfied by the short gasps of breath.

Then there was a gentle touch on her shoulder and a warmth at her back.

"Runa," Keshin's deep voice said.

His tone was soothing in a way she'd never heard from him before. He shifted her to a kneeling position then crouched in front of her, trailing his hand from her back, to her shoulder, down her arm to gather her hands in his, placing one to his chest and one to hers.

"Breathe with me."

Runa's eyes focused on the center of Keshin's chest where he held their hands. The expansive plain moved with his inhale, and Runa did her best to do the same.

Keshin exhaled, and Runa copied him.

Once calm, Keshin gathered her into his arms. "I have you."

She felt like she was going to shake out of his embrace. Keshin cradled her close to his chest, his warmth seeping into her.

Runa barely registered that they were moving. The camp and soldiers were a blur of color as Keshin carried her the short distance back to her tent.

They're probably staring at me, thinking I'm a mess, she thought. The healer who can't handle death.

Like she's weak.

She should protest, tell Keshin to put her down. But Runa wasn't in any condition to stand, let alone walk.

Her breathing was rapid and shallow, skin cool and clammy, her heartbeat rapid. Then there was the dizziness, the disorientation, the nausea.

Keshin lowered her onto a soft mat with blankets that felt familiar. He brought her back to her tent.

"I have to leave," Runa said.

"You're in no state to go anywhere."

"They'll come for you again."

Runa doubted there was a safe place for her. Keshin would probably turn her out now rather than risk his death.

Keshin grabbed her chin between his thumb and forefinger, then tilted her head up. She looked at him as if she was seeing him for the first time. His hair was unbound and hung down around his face.

"You are safe," he said. His beautiful eyes stared into Runa's, making sure she felt the weight of his words.

And in that moment, she knew those words to be true. Runa knew in her soul that nothing would come to harm her while Keshin was there.

The moment passed as Keshin went to stand. Before she realized what happened, Runa's hand shot out to grab his arm.

"Don't leave," she said.

Keshin took her hand in his, bringing it to his mouth. "Never."

He called for more guards, his voice booming through the camp. It caused Runa to jump, but she knew in her core that Keshin would not hurt her.

A few moments later, two men scrambled inside the tent.

"Secure the camp. Find any remaining intruders. I want them alive so I can take their heads." Keshin asked.

Both bowed in reverence. "Anything else, my lord?"

"Bring clean water to my tent for Lady Runa."

The two men nodded and left. An undetermined amount of time later, two servants brought in the buckets of warm water, placing it in the center of her tent. Two female attendants entered and bowed, keeping their eyes pinned on the ground, waiting for orders.

"Leave us," Keshin said.

Everyone bowed again and exited the tent, leaving Runa and Keshin alone.

He turned to her and in the most gentle voice she had ever heard said, "Let me undress you."

"I can bathe myself," she said weakly. It was just a bucket of warm water and a sponge.

He pressed his forehead against hers, cupping her face with his hands.

"I know," Keshin whispered. "It is my honor to do this for you."

Slowly, his touch drifted from her jaw, down her neck to her shoulders. His fingers trailed down her arms, then his hands gathered the bloodied sleeping garment and peeled it off of her and over her head.

Somehow, undressing in front of Keshin was more vulnerable than killing a man in front of him. Runa had never been more exposed in her life—naked in front of the most dangerous man in the land.

But she never felt more protected.

And she was grateful for his attention. She didn't want to be alone right now.

Keshin gathered her in his arms again and led her to a stool by the bucket of water. Before he started, Keshin shed his shirt, and for the first time, Runa felt like she truly saw Keshin. Not as a warlord, not as the Senshin, but as a man.

He was solely focused on her. She raised her left hand to place it on his chest. He grasped her hand in his, thumb tracing over Runa's Unmei mark.

"You came for me," he said.

"This told me," she responded, tracing his Unmei mark, the physical representation of their bond forever inked on their skin. "I felt you use my power."

"You saved my life," Keshin admitted. "My life is yours."

"How did you do it?"

"Aylis," he said. Then added, "I heard a woman's voice telling me what to do. A voice not unlike yours."

Runa registered the words, but was unsettled by the depth of their meaning. Somehow, he was able to tap into Aylis's power without her. And when Runa saw Keshin in trouble she was able to tap into Tharaveld's power.

But now their powers were switched, and they had no idea for how long, nor how to switch them back.

Keshin grabbed the soap and sponge, lathering them together, then slid it along her skin. He paid exceptional attention, moving the sponge between her fingers, up her arm and back down to repeat. Runa was transfixed by the motion.

Between the water and Keshin's ministrations, Runa did her best to relax. Every pass of the sponge sent her further into a trance.

Then he washed her hair, and his fingers felt divine against her scalp.

"You don't have to do this," Runa said as he rinsed her hair.

"I want to," Keshin's low voice rumbled, sending Runa's heart racing for an entirely different reason.

Because something in her needed him, his presence, his steadiness, the gentleness that existed beneath his calloused hands. She didn't understand it. Didn't know if she wanted to. This wasn't how she was supposed to feel about him.

And yet, with each pass of the cloth, her chest ached with something she couldn't name. He looked at her like she was more than a weapon, more than a pawn, more than a burden bound to him by divine decree.

It scared her, how he touched her now, not with hunger or ownership, but with reverence. Like every inch of her body deserved remembering. Like this night made her braver, not broken.

Runa told herself Keshin was a brute. He only tolerated her because the gods said he must. But what if she'd been wrong? What if, despite the gods, he would *choose* her of his own volition?

Heat rushed to her core. She didn't understand it. This man who terrified the world held her like glass, guarded her like a fortress, and now touched her as if she were something precious. In this moment, with his fingers trailing over her, she allowed herself to close her eyes, just for a second, and feel safe.

And that, more than anything, unsettled her.

Still, she allowed herself to sink into him.

He withdrew from the water and fetched a towel for her. Runa took her time getting her footing and stepping into the cloth. He pulled the towel around her, dried her off, and dressed her in a fresh nightgown of his colors.

"I shouldn't be wearing this," she said.

"Runa," Keshin's voice was stern, but not unkind. "You are mine. Mine to care for, mine to protect. You more than anyone deserve to wear my colors and sleep by my side."

Waves of emotion ran through her. Relief, confusion, embarrassment, and something else. A sense of safety and security.

Once again, Keshin picked up Runa and carried her back to her bed. Runa didn't object. When he turned to leave, Runa grabbed his hand.

"Stay with me," she said, not sure if it was a request or a plea.

The ghost of a smile passed over his mouth as he said, "let me clean myself first."

Keshin methodically removed his blood soaked clothes, exposing his muscles beneath. Runa had seen naked men before, but she had never seen one like Keshin. His body was carved from years of dedication to his craft, all hard lines and sculpted strength. His muscles shifted like the tide beneath his sun-kissed skin. She followed the lines of him, the way his physique tightened and flexed with even the smallest movement, effortless yet commanding.

Her eyes lingered lower, drinking in the tautness of his waist, the way his back narrowed before flaring out into the lean strength of his hips. Every inch of him was built for control, precision—a force that could be gentle or devastating, depending on his intent.

And now, he was intent on her.

He bathed quickly, just enough to wash the blood from his body. When he was done, he called for the guards to remove the water and dressed in clean clothes before slipping into the bed beside her.

Gathering Runa into his arms he said, "You are not a burden."

The words were spoken into her hair, but she felt them pierce her heart like a blade.

"I bring more death to people than I do good," Runa said, voice trembling. And tonight she had taken her first life.

"You did what you had to do to protect your life. And mine," Keshin said.

But it was more than that.

"Death follows me like a vengeful spirit. Just as many people have died trying to protect me, save me, as I have helped."

"You blame yourself for the greed of men," Keshin said.

"Isaku and Akio died protecting me." Tears ran in rivulets down her cheeks.

"Isaku is not dead yet. But if he does not die today, he could die on the battlefield a week from now. You do not know what fates the gods have devised for them."

Runa never thought about it like that. But she couldn't shake the guilt that Aiko had given his life in protecting her.

"You inspire hope in a way that I never will," Keshin said.

"Now who is lying to themselves?" Runa asked. "I've seen the hope you invoke in your men."

She felt Keshin's whole body move. His arms curled around her, pulling her into his chest. Runa never felt as safe as she did with this man. Maybe that's why Aylis and Tharveld brought them together. Keshin had the power to keep her safe, and Runa's abilities could heal his wounds.

"Don't leave me alone," Runa whispered.

Then she felt him press a kiss to the top of her head.

"Never," Keshin promised.

Chapter 8

R una stirred beneath the layers of blankets, the scent of crushed herbs and blood still clinging faintly to the air. Her body ached. Her mind drifted. Memories of the night before flickered through her. Steel glinting in the moonlight, the snap of—

"Toraichi has accepted your challenge," a man said. Hoshi, Keshin's second.

The warmth at her side stirred. She watched the curve of his back, the tension in his shoulders, the way his hand paused slightly when he realized she was awake too.

He had stayed with her. Not for duty. Because she asked, and he chose to.

"Keshin," she said.

He turned, familiar mahogany eyes sharp but softened at the edges when they landed on her.

"What does he mean? Who accepted your challenge?"

Attendants entered the tent and Keshin shifted to block her from view. But not before Runa caught the lacquered plates of armor in their hands.

"Torachi must pay for his transgressions," Keshin said as if it were that simple.

"So you challenged him to what? A duel?"

Keshin nodded once, then broke their eye contact to don his underclothes.

He's going to do what now? They had just been attacked. Keshin almost died last night. He must have sent a messenger in the middle of the night.

"Everyone get out!" Runa sat up, holding the blanket to her chest.

Thankfully, the attendants and soldiers listened to her, immediately stopping their tasks and leaving the tent without a second glance at Keshin.

But as everyone left, Keshin's mahogany eyes were glaring at her, branding her. His brow lowered, his posture rigid.

Runa pulled the fabric around her, uncomfortable under the intensity of his gaze. Not that modesty mattered much after he had bathed every inch of her.

"You've challenged Toraichi to single combat?"

Keshin nodded. "He's accepted my challenge."

"And none of that seems suspicious to you?"

This was the same man who sent his second to the peace talks so he could investigate her abilities as the Iyashite. The same man who sent assassins in the dead of night to kill Keshin.

"He will answer for his offenses," Keshin said.

Runa rose from the bed, bringing the blanket with her. "He has no honor, Keshin."

"Then the gods will favor us and he will die."

"Toraichi would never willingly choose to challenge the Senshin without knowing he had the upper hand."

"I am prepared."

Runa's eyes narrowed at her bonded. "Channel."

"What?"

"Channel Tharaveld's power." She stood firm, arms gripping the fabric tightly.

Keshin's nostrils flared as he exhaled sharply, his annoyance evident. Still, he acquiesced and his eyes closed. Her foot tapped a rhythm as she waited for him to realize what she already suspected.

When he opened his eyes, they were turquoise, the same as last night.

"You can't channel." Runa's voice wavered.

And if he can't channel ... Runa closed her eyes, reaching for Aylis's light within her. The space it normally occupied felt like a dark, bottomless hole.

"I can't feel her," she said, her voice barely a whisper.

"It doesn't matter."

Those were not the words Runa wanted to hear.

Runa extended her arms out to her sides, letting the sheet fall to the floor. "What do you mean it doesn't matter? You can't channel Tharaveld's power right now. And I don't feel Aylis."

Keshin's mouth fell open but he quickly caught himself, running his hand over the lower half of his face. "You think I am a child that is so easily beaten? For as long as you trained as a healer, I've trained longer as a warrior. Since I was a child."

Her hands clenched into fists as she began to shake and she felt anger course through her. How could he not understand how dangerous this was?

Keshin closed the distance between them, cupping her face with his hands. "You are worried." A sparkle of something glimmered behind his eyes.

The warmth of his skin soothed the tension. "It's not your skill I'm worried about," Runa said.

"Do you know how many men I could not bring back from death's door, who thought just like you? I have seen the trickery of dishonorable men."

Runa took in his tall posture, the set of his shoulders, and knew there was no changing his mind. He was going to do this whether she liked it or not. Runa wasn't sure if it was confidence or pride driving this desire.

"If I can't channel, I can't heal you. If–"

"You're staying here."

His words sent a jolt up her spine, causing it to straighten. She removed herself from his grip and gave him a firm stare. "I'm coming with you."

"No. A woman—"

"This woman you're divinely bound to will not sit and wait for you to return while our powers are switched." The sentence came out a little more forceful than she intended, but it caused him to freeze and stop speaking.

Runa withdrew from Keshin's touch and walked over to the trunk of clothes, rummaging until she found a simple shirt and loose pants, similar to what a soldier would wear under their armor.

"You could get hurt," he protested.

"So could you." She sent him a scowl before putting on the pants.

"Toraichi could capture you."

"If you are so confident in your abilities then make sure that doesn't happen," she reasoned. "Besides, if we can switch powers, then maybe you can pull on Tharaveld's power from me. Or maybe I can push it into you."

"Do you know how to do that?" Keshin asked, leveling a harsh stare at her.

No, she didn't, but Runa only shrugged. She felt like the tentative truce between them was fading like night into the dawn. They had only just learned that they could switch powers. Channeling one power through their divine bond didn't seem like too far-fetched an idea.

There was a scratching noise at the tent's opening and Keshin's second, Hoshi, walked through. His salt and pepper hair was pulled back into a bun. Hoshi was fully dressed in his armor, but there was a faded scar that marred the right side of his jawline.

Hoshi bowed to both Runa and Keshin. "My lord Senshin, Lady Runa, the horses are ready."

Keshin's mouth pulled into a thin line. "Lady Runa will be joining us."

"Toraichi could steal her Lord Senshin," Hoshi cautioned.

"He can try," Runa mumbled.

Keshin grunted some version of a laugh, then addressed Hoshi. "If I fall, you take her and you flee."

Hoshi bowed again. "Of course, my lord."

"Runa, you will go with him without question or complaint."

That was a big ask, even for him. Runa nibbled the bottom of her lip as the weight of his request washed over her.

"You won't fall, not today, not by his hand," Runa said.

Blanketed in darkness, the trio moved through the camp to the temporary stable where three horses and another official waited. Runa didn't bother asking about a horse for herself. She approached the black stallion. Keshin's hands gripped her waist, hoisting her onto the horse's back, before he swung up behind her.

The sun bathed the sky in brilliant golds and rich persimmons as Keshin's small procession approached the outskirts of the town. It was still early enough that most people would be sleeping. Hoshi flanked him on the right and a small entourage of three soldiers followed behind. Each carried their katana and wakizashi short sword on their hip. The duel was to take place at the same location as the peace talks, just outside the town.

As they rode, Runa leaned into Keshin's chest, trying to focus on their Unmei, the divine connection between them. She felt the tug of the thread that connected them. Pulling on their connection was not the same as activating Tharaveld's power, and channeling was still completely different than pushing that power down the bond or reaching down the thread to access the other's power.

Toraichi was already waiting for them as they arrived at the slapdash ring. Like Keshin, he too had a small retinue.

"His sword looks strange." Like a katana, but with an extra long handle.

"It's called a nagamaki and is used for cutting down mounted riders," Keshin explained. Pulling back on the reins, the horse came to a stop. Keshin dismounted then turned, placing both hands on Runa's waist to help her off the horse.

Yet he didn't let go, even when she was safely on the ground. Instead, he stepped closer, placing his forehead on hers. "Remember what I told you."

Runa was taken by surprise by the tender action. She wouldn't have thought Keshin would show such emotion before a fight. Then again, these could be his last moments and this was what he needed, this connection with her.

Not knowing what else to do, she lifted her hands to either side of his face. "You will not fall today," Runa repeated.

When he broke away he turned towards Hoshi, placing a hand on the elder man's shoulders. Something unspoken passed between the two men, then Hoshi bowed. "The honor is mine, Lord Senshin."

Without another word, Keshin gave them his back and walked toward what was supposed to be a location for peace, but now was a bare trodden patch of dirt where the tents once stood.

Toraichi, too, left the safety of his men and stepped towards the ring.

"I was surprised to get your request," Toraichi said, holding the hilt of the long blade outstretched in front of him. That weapon was the only thing protecting him from Keshin's fury.

"I don't trust this," Runa whispered to Hoshi. She wasn't convinced that this bastard wouldn't try to pull some trick.

"Neither do I, my lady," Hoshi said.

At least she wasn't the only one.

Keshin drew his blade and took a fighting stance.

"Thanks for bringing her. You've saved me the effort of tracking her down later."

Even from her position, Runa saw the way Toraichi's mouth twisted in a malicious grin. Unbothered by the taunt, Keshin stood tall, his eyes trained on the enemy. Unlike her bonded, Runa could not help the barb that spewed forth. "You possess a serpent's tongue and venom for a soul."

"I will enjoy watching the life drain from your eyes." Keshin said, as he rushed at Toraichi, his sword pulled back.

Runa's heart dropped into her stomach as Torachi swung his giant sword in a sweeping arc, slashing at Keshin's stomach. A cry lodged in the back of her throat as her hands flew to her mouth. Keshin brought his katana down in time to block the attack.

The weight of Hoshi's hand appeared on her shoulder. "Steel yourself, Lady Runa."

Runa only nodded as her eyes remained fixed on the two warlords and their dance for dominance. They moved with precision and grace. Runa should have expected that from warriors who have trained for duels to the death.

Toraichi made large sweeping movements to keep Keshin away, while her bonded tried to find opportunities to get in close. Runa was transfixed by the way Keshin moved. He was an artist. The ring was his canvas, and the sword his brush. He painted lines of sparks as metal clashed. And this was without Tharaveld's power coursing through him.

The next clash of metal shook Runa out of her thoughts. She was supposed to be trying to channel Tharaveld's power. Channeling Aylis's gifts required a clear, calm mind. Runa pictured the task she wanted to perform and let Aylis's power flow through her. Maybe it was the same for Tharaveld's.

Except, she wasn't exactly paying attention to *how* she tapped into the power when she beheaded the assassin.

Her attention was pulled back to the fight as Toraichi made another downward slash, causing Keshin to back away. However, Toraichi's foot slipped on a rock throwing off his balance. Both men saw the mistake and Keshin darted for the other warlord.

Runa's heart hammered in her chest. This was it, the duel was over. As Keshin rushed forward, Toraichi's second entered the field, katana brandished and aimed at Keshin's back.

Fear spiked through Runa as she called out, "Behind you!"

Keshin ducked and twisted out of the reach of the two men. Unconsciously, Runa stepped forward, as if her muscles knew what they had to do. Hoshi's hand on her shoulder held her back.

"Go and help him," Runa begged the elder warrior.

Hoshi shook his head. "That would not be honorable. The Senshin would not want to sink to their level of deceitfulness to win this battle."

It was painful to watch Keshin exchange blows with the second while being mindful of the nagamaki's range. She watched her face turning white. Yet with every clash of their steel, Runa felt her muscles vibrate with excitement.

Keshin spun out of the way of another strike of Toraichi's weapon and rotated his body behind the second, slicing down his back. The second fell to the ground writhing in pain.

Once again it was one on one. Keshin pivoted to face his opponent, and Runa could see the sweat rolling down his face and light of exhilaration in his gaze as he held his katana out.

The two lunged at each other and Runa felt a rush of energy surged through her as she watched.

Was that the key? Runa wondered. The lust of battle that fueled Tharaveld's power?

Closing her eyes, she searched for the genesis of that feeling, replaying the sequence of blows in her mind. Adrenaline pulsed through her, and her body screamed at her to enter the duel.

She knew nothing of combat, but with this feeling coursing through her, she felt like she could fight.

Her gaze returned to the duel as Keshin advanced on Toriachi, whose movements now seemed lethargic, the speed at which he swung the nagamaki slowed.

"Lady Runa, your eyes ... they're red." Hoshi said.

This was it, the way to tap into Tharaveld's power, but how could she push it through the bond?

"Ah!" Toraichi cried out, drawing Runa's attention back to the battle.

Keshin stood over the other man, twisting Toraichi's right arm so the other warlord was forced to release his grip on the nagamaki and fell to his knees.

"Any last words?" Keshin asked as he held his katana to Toraichi's neck.

"Die," Toraichi spat.

In the moment of silence before Toraichi's death, Runa heard the familiar twang of a bow, the whistle of an arrow flying through the air. The thud as the projectile embedded itself in Keshin's chestplate. Runa knew by the depth of the exposed shaft that the arrow had pierced through the armor and was embedded somewhere in Keshin's ribs. A fatal wound, or it would be if he couldn't channel Aylis's blessing.

She had barely processed this first projectile when another pierced his shoulder, and a third in his leg. Keshin stumbled back a few steps. Runa looked around, trying to pinpoint their source as a fourth arrow punctured Keshin's abdomen. A fifth and sixth arrow soon followed.

Her legs screamed at her to run to him. She could save him—no, she couldn't. Runa didn't have her healing powers.

All she could do was stand back and watch as the seventh and eighth arrows pierced him.

Rage consumed Runa as she watched Toraichi stand, retrieve his blade, and stalk towards Keshin, who was gasping for air. Katana still in hand, Keshin dropped to his knees. Toraichi held up his hand and the volley stopped.

"You thought your power made you invincible, Senshin. But who has the power now?"

He was going to die, Toraichi was going to kill him. She had to do something.

"I want you to know, I'll enjoy killing you." Toraichi said.

She couldn't let that happen.

Runa shrugged off Hoshi's hold and sprinted toward the men. If the warlords noticed her, they did nothing to stop her as she barreled into Keshin. The blade came down, slicing white hot rays of fire across her back. She let out a piercing cry.

Her knees gave out and she fell to the ground, her arms catching her. Pain pounded through her back and seized her thoughts as something warm, thick, and wet soaked her clothes.

Blood.

Her blood.

Toraichi stumbled back, away from her and Keshin. "You stupid girl!"

Runa writhed in pain, rolling on the ground, trying to find a position that did not cause hot spikes of pain to shoot through her limbs.

A blurry figure entered her limited field of vision. It leaned down over her.

"How do I heal you?" the figure asked, his voice laced with desperation.

She would know his voice anywhere.

"Keshin ... clear ... mind." Runa tried to form words between groans of pain. Trails of tears stained her face.

She felt so cold, her body began to shake. Runa needed healing now. Maybe she could draw it from Keshin the way he did from her. Focusing on the thread between them, she imagined she was pulling herself along the bond like she was crawling along a precarious parapet.

Runa felt the soothing power of Aylis's blessing radiating the further she crawled away from her pain.

"Aylis," the words fell from her lips. "Please."

Her answer was the distant clash of metal and an angry roar.

"You will not die today," someone called in a voice deep, commanding, and guttural.

Don't give me orders, she tried to sass, but the words came out in a moan of pain. Her lips wouldn't move and her tongue felt heavy in her mouth. Cold. She was so cold.

The last thing she felt was the warm embrace of Aylis's light flowing into her body before everything went black.

Chapter 9

Death's embrace felt like the sun on Runa's skin. She floated on her back in a sea, rocking her gently as a baby, calming her spirit. Runa let the watery abyss sway her gently as she drifted, unbothered by the approaching island in the distance. Something told her she wanted to go to this land. There, her soul would want for not. There, she could finally rest.

No more running, no more suffering. Just tranquility calling her to its shores.

Runa was about to succumb to the serenity of the tide when a voice cut through the lull of the waves.

"Runa," the familiar timbre whispered as if it was speaking to a lover.

"Keshin," she said, her voice garbled, as if she were under water, yet she could breathe just fine.

Moving her arms through the liquid, Runa tried to find balance as she shifted her weight from lying on her back to an upright position. She found more resistance than she expected, as if the current didn't want her to move. It wanted her to remain prone in the waves, to let them carry her to her final destination.

"Stay with me." Keshin's desperation broke through the void again.

I'm here, she wanted to say, but she couldn't find the words. Language was fading into the distance along with her will to fight the tide.

Runa reached for the string of fate that connected her to Keshin, tried to grasp its frayed strands to speak to him, but nothing came. The string was stretched too thin, too weak to do anything but exist.

"Runa, don't go. Come back to me," Keshin coaxed her. "I don't want to lose you."

He didn't want to lose her. She turned the words over in her mind. Her? Or her power? Their interactions had been less than civil during most of their time together. She had refused to heal him the night they first met, though she healed his grievously injured men. But he never treated her poorly. He respected her, even if he didn't fully understand her power. Keshin had provided what she asked for, and things she didn't even know she wanted.

Realization dawned. Her assumptions about Keshin were entirely wrong. He wasn't a mindless bloodthirsty warmonger. He would rather sacrifice himself than send his men into battle. He was the type of person who took care of the people around him.

Including her.

The truth was, Runa didn't *want* to leave him.

She looked back to the island with an overwhelming sense of dread. At that moment, Runa understood that if she set foot on its shores, she would never see Keshin again.

Kicking her feet furiously, she fought against the current. But despite her efforts, she didn't feel like she was getting anywhere.

"I want to go back," Runa said between breaths.

Stay, the water seemed to say.

Aylis, Runa prayed. *Help me get back to him.*

The water around her heated to the same familiar warmth she felt when she was healing. The dark depths around her slowly brightened from an inky blue black to a brilliant turquoise.

Her eyes flew open as she tried to sit up. She wasn't swimming anymore. Instead a pair of strong arms cradled her while two red eyes dominated her vision.

She was back in the village. Well, that wasn't entirely right. She was in Keshin's arms. Tucked close to his body as one large hand cupped her face.

"Runa," Keshin said in a breathy voice. "You came back."

She tried to speak, but her words were silenced as his mouth descended on hers in gentle kiss, a single moment stretched over infinity.

At first, she didn't understand what was happening. Runa had never known the feeling of someone else's lips, but with Keshin's mouth on hers, she felt like she could soar. Her hands reached for him, grasping at his chest plate so she could hold herself to him. But as soon as she recognized what was going on, Keshin pulled back.

He still held her in his arms, but barked orders to his second. "Send word back to camp. Have the tents and an elite unit moved here."

"My lord," Hoshi's voice laced with caution. "What about Toraichi's men?"

"Round up his commanding officers. I will deal with them after I'm satisfied that my bonded is secure."

Hoshi nodded and left the two of them alone.

"You can put me down now," Runa said, shifting in his arms, testing the stiff muscles and noting the dull throb of pain. At least it wasn't the sharp searing pain of a fresh wound.

"I know." The corner of Keshin's mouth turned upward, but he made no move to release her from the his embrace.

Her heart skipped a beat at the smirk, at the banter that was not lost between them despite their near death experiences.

"Must I repeat myself?"

A muscle next to his crimson eye twitched.

"Let me care for you, Runa." His voice was uncharacteristically tender.

"You don't have to."

The words were out of her mouth before she could think. Runa wondered why that was her automatic response. She spent so much time taking care of other people. Had she forgotten how to let other people care for her?

Keshin's fingers traced from her hairline, down the side of her face, to her jaw where he hooked the digit under her chin, encouraging her to look up at him.

"It is my honor and pleasure to do so."

Heat flooded her cheeks as her heart pounded in her chest. What was she supposed to do with a statement like that? There was an intimacy there that she didn't know how to handle. Runa turned her face into Keshin's chest to hide the blush.

"Fine," she relented. "Just to make you feel useful."

Even though she felt the familiar warm pulse of Aylis's power, she was too drained to channel. Runa's whole body felt heavy, like she had walked all day. Each breath was a struggle, fatigue settled within her like silt in a riverbed.

Keshin's torso rumbled with laughter.

"Your eyes, you're channeling Tharaveld," Runa commented, recalling his red eyes and feeling her connection to Aylis again.

Keshin nodded. "Something snapped when I saw you take the blow for me."

"Did you kill him?"

"Hoshi did. Ran him through before Toraichi could take off our heads."

"Good." Piece of shit deserved it.

They must have been such a sight. The two of them, covered with blood, with the dead bodies of Toriachi and his second lying a few feet away. Yet amidst the violence, Keshin held Runa as if she were the most precious thing in the world. Not because she was fragile, but because he wanted to.

Runa didn't know what to do with that sentiment. Another thought crossed her mind.

"How are you healed?" She turned her face to look at him. Not a single arrow protruded from his body.

"You did it, right before you opened your eyes."

When her brows furrowed. Keshin continued, "I was calling out to you, but you were fading. But after a while, you started glowing. Not just your eyes, but your entire body. You healed both of us."

"I was floating in this body of water, drifting toward some land, when I heard you call out to me. Then I was trying to swim, fighting the current. I called out to Aylis for help and it was like she lifted me out of the water. That's when I opened my eyes and saw you."

"You came back for me?"

Runa was silent for a moment, wondering if she wanted to admit the truth to him. Doing so meant something between them had changed irrevocably. The truth was that she would have drifted to that shore if not for his voice. And it was her desire to get to Keshin that spurred her life.

Runa nodded once.

Keshin beamed at her, eyes wide and glowing, like the morning sun was rising behind them.

She wasn't sure what the fluttering sensation was in her stomach, or why her eyes focused on the curve of his mouth. She hoped he would kiss her.

And holy Aylis blessing, as if he could read her thoughts he leaned down and kissed her. Keshin pressed his mouth to hers in front of Hoshi and who knows how many others. Being cradled in Keshin's embrace limited her view of the field around them. The intimacy was overwhelming. She pulled away, flushed and tried to reclaim something more familiar between them.

"You're predisposed to injury and near-death experiences. Of course I had to come back," she said, using the quip to mask the feelings she wasn't yet ready to admit to him.

Keshin smirked and shook his head, as if he was amused by her comment, the glow fading from his eyes.

The Senshin continued to hold his Iyashite right there in the makeshift battle ring. No more words passed between them until a squad of men bearing supplies for the tent arrived. They built the structure around where Keshin held Runa.

With the tent erected, and a semblance of privacy, Keshin rose to his feet before cautiously transferring Runa from his arms to the bed. Her stiff muscles protested as the pain throbbed like a steady drum beat.

Keshin rummaged through her things to produce a piece of white willow bark. "I'll have them make some tea for you."

He remembered what the bark was used for and knew it could help ease her pain. Damn that fluttering feeling was back.

Thankfully, there was scratching at the outside of the tent and Hoshi entered, bowing to both of them. "My lord, Torachi's officers have been rounded up."

Keshin nodded at his second then turned back to Runa. "I need to deal with the rest of Toraichi's army."

"What will you do?" she asked shifting to make herself comfortable.

He hesitated, then reluctantly said, "What honor demands."

Once, she might have thought Keshin relished in this part of war. Now she knew better. He dreaded it. She could see it in the slump of his shoulders, the way his mouth turned down. These men could be honorable men, good men, but loyal to the wrong lord. Some will choose to die by their own hand, others imprisoned, most put to work in the lower ranks. So was the way of Keshin's world: brutal. But this was how he protected the lives of so many others.

"Show mercy?" Runa asked, holding his mahogany stare.

Keshin nodded once then said, "Sleep. The war is over. We can go home."

Keshin left the tent, giving express orders to the guards at the entrance about who was and was not allowed to attend to her.

As she fell asleep, Runa reflected on the word "home," the implications. It had been years since she could use that word to refer to such a place, or maybe home wasn't a place for her. Maybe home was with Keshin.

But what did that mean for their relationship moving forward? Something shifted, she could tell that much. She came back for him, would he have done the same for her? The way he recounted the events, it seemed like he was only concerned with her when Toraichi sliced open her back. It angered him so much that he channeled Tharaveld's power once again. She recalled the pleading sound in Keshin's voice as she floated in that ethereal body of water. How he pleaded. Did that mean he didn't want her to go either?

These feelings were so confusing.

Time passed in long stretches of sleep interspersed with her attendants slipping in and out of the tent to bring her tea, food, and water to wash. When Keshin returned he personally tended to her needs, feeding her, bathing her like he did before, and holding her when she drifted back to sleep.

Runa didn't know how he found the time to care for her and attend to his duties, taking care of the remnants of Toraichi's army. Keshin awarded Toraichi's lands to men loyal to him and the faction took off to secure the lands.

When Runa could stand and walk without significant amounts of pain, Keshin gave the order to return to their homeland. Their detachment reunited with their greater battalion, including the new additions from Toraichi's army. The scouts were ordered to ride out ahead as the rest of the army readied themselves for travel.

Runa's attendants packed her things well and placed them on a wagon, which she refused to ride in. Just because she almost died didn't mean she had to be locked away in a cage for her protection. Instead, she marched over to her horse and swung up without assistance from anyone. Admittedly, it was a stupid thing to do because a jolt of pain shot up her back where she knew the scar from Toraichi's blow had landed.

When her bodyguards looked toward Keshin for help, he only chuckled and spurred on his horse.

With a smirk Runa pressed the heel of her foot into the horse's side, urging it forward. It listened to her, but she was unable to catch up with Keshin before Hoshi, and the other commanding officers fell in next to him.

Keshin made no order to allow room for her next to him, and something didn't settle right in her chest. He spent the last three days and nights at her side, as if he would die before he let someone else come between them.

It felt strange to be separated from him, like a part of her was missing.

Wait, when did she start seeking out Keshin as a source of comfort?

Was she reading the situation wrong? Maybe that was only because they both almost died. She had never been in a moving warband before, there was probably a protocol she didn't know.

But she was the Iyashite, bonded to the Senshin. Surely she outranked everyone else.

"Move," she ordered.

"Lady Runa?" one of her new bodyguards asked. Tadashi if she recalled correctly. Names were still hard for her to learn. She was better with faces.

"Were your ears damaged in the battle? Do I need to heal them?"

"No ma'am."

"Then move out of my way."

Runa spurred her horse forward, the others parted for her as various calls of "clear a path" rang out. She disregarded the shocked look of the officers as she rode up to Keshin's left side then pulled on the reins to match the speed of his horse.

"Would you like to learn to wield a blade?"

His question gave Runa pause. "You would teach me how to fight?"

"Teach you how to block an attack with something other than your body, yes."

Runa did not, could not, stop the smile that overtook her. "I'd like that."

"When we return and you are settled in our home, then we will find you a tutor."

How could he say "our home" so casually like it didn't mean everything to her that she would have somewhere to rest, to lay her head, people to help, without the constant fear of abduction looming over her.

That night, there was only one tent erected for them to share. And when Keshin came to bed, he pulled Runa into his side where she curled against the heat of his body. Her head lay on his chest where his robe parted, revealing the hard planes of his chest. She felt so cherished by the simple gesture.

Runa breathed in the woodsy scent of him and pressed as much of her body against his, like she couldn't get close enough. She had never felt this way before about any man.

Was this what it felt like when a woman desired a man? The better question was, did Keshin feel the same?

Chapter 10

D ays passed and the landscape of Oshiren shifted from mountains to dense forest, into serene rice paddies and small villages. Inhabitants lined their modest streets waving and sneaking glimpses at their lord as the army marched past.

Throughout it all, Keshin told stories about the time he spent in this town or that, helping people and learning the land. He too was from a small village, not unlike the ones they passed. Not unlike the one where Runa grew up.

"My sword master lived there," Keshin pointed to a homestead off their path.

"I bet you were the best student," Runa jested.

Keshin laughed, a beautiful, deep sound from his belly. "At ten years old, I thought I knew everything. I was young and headstrong. I wanted to practice with the older kids. Hoshi was the first to humble me."

She enjoyed learning more about Keshin. Enjoyed spending time with him without the looming threat of Toraichi. It was like they were learning about each other in a way they couldn't before.

"When did you become a lord?" Runa asked.

"Two years after Tharaveld's blessing manifested. I was an officer in my lord's army. When he learned of my blessing, he ordered me to assassinate his political rival."

His eyebrows furrow, his expression pained. Asking him to do something so young, Runa just shook her head. It was disgusting. Just like Toraichi sent shinobi in the dead of night to eliminate Keshin and kidnap her.

"So, what did you do?" she asked.

"I left his service, along with a significant number of others. Hoshi was one of them. He tempered me a lot in those early years. I thought I was untouchable."

Runa pictured a younger, dashing Keshin riding over the hills like the land was all his own. He had every chance to become a tyrant, but somehow didn't.

"What did you do after you left?"

"We helped towns and villages in return for food. We hunted down bandits. Protected local figures against mercenaries, but only if we deemed them honorable."

"What about your lord?"

"He never gave up trying to kill me, so we met on the battlefield."

Runa could guess how that battle ended.

The long days of riding wore on Runa. She wasn't used to riding on horseback all day. They stayed in towns overnight when they could. With each stop, Runa would heal those in need before retiring. Then, she would let the warmth of Aylis's power soothe her aching muscles.

Keshin would enter sometime later, sliding between the sheets and pulling her close to him. Despite the growing connection between them, he never did anything more than hold her. And Runa didn't understand why. Did he not feel the pull between them? Briefly, she entertained the idea of asking one of her female attendants how to proposition a man. But her tongue twisted, the words unable to form as color stained her cheeks to the point they thought she was sick.

And so their days passed.

After two weeks of travel, Keshin pointed to a city on the horizon and said, "We're almost there." Runa thought she grew up in a city, but it was nothing compared to Keshin's. Everywhere she looked, people were stacked on top of each other. Their parade meandered down streets lined with colorful lanterns and streamers while people tossed flower petals that fell down like the gentle spring rains. It was clear that Keshin was as beloved as he was powerful.

Curious eyes appraised her as she rode next to their revered ruler. Some people whispered behind fans as their eyes flicked over Runa. Others brazenly pointed and called out. "That must be her!"

Their procession through the streets was slow, but eventually they approached the sweeping expanse of his palace like a beautiful oasis. Extensive gardens wove through a fortified center that housed adjoining administrative buildings and the living quarters for Keshin's soldiers and household staff.

Stable hands met them in the courtyard to steady the horses.

"Stay," Keshin ordered as Runa went to dismount.

Her immediate reaction was to disobey. She had been getting on and off her horse just fine these last three months. But they weren't on the road, they were surrounded by judgemental gazes assessing her every move. Her posture went rigid and she shifted in her seat as she fixed her gaze on her bonded. Keshin approached the left side of her horse. His hands found her waist. She leaned into him and placed her hands on his shoulders to steady herself as he helped her dismount.

When her feet were planted safely on the ground, Keshin leaned down so his mouth was next to her ear.

"Welcome home," he whispered.

Her heart skipped a beat and his warm breath caressed her skin, sending a shiver up her spine. She'd swear to Aylis she felt the feather light touch of his lips on her cheek as he straightened and placed one hand on her lower back, ushering her toward the front of the palace.

Runa lifted her chin and stared ahead at the lines of attendants flanking the stairs. They bowed deeply as the pair ascended. Her eyes landed on a woman at the top dressed in Keshin's house colors of red and black.

She looked older than Runa, dark hair pulled back tight to the base of her head, secured with a beautiful crystal headpiece.

Who was this woman?

With every step, Runa's breaths came quicker and shallower. Not because she had difficulty climbing the steps, but because adrenaline shots through her system. She stood in a storm of stares, each one measuring, questioning, deciding what to make of her. And this woman's gaze was at the center.

Runa's eyes flicked between Keshin and the woman. They had the same proud nose, same high cheekbones and almond-shaped eyes. Not that Runa spent a lot of time looking at Keshin's features. Definitely not in the early hours of the morning when the sunlight painted his face in shades of gold.

When they reached the top of the stairs, the woman bowed. "Brother, the gods have blessed us with your return," she greeted.

Brother?

"It's good to be home, sister," Keshin returned a slight bow.

She let out a breath and sent a silent prayer up to Aylis as relief sunk in.

When he straightened, Keshin extended a hand to Runa, welcoming her forward. "May I introduce Aylis's Iyashite, Lady Runa. Runa, this is my sister, Lady Miwa."

Runa smiled softly and bowed to Miwa. "It is a pleasure to meet you."

Miwa returned the gesture. "The pleasure is mine, Iyashite."

"Please call me Runa."

Miwa looked to Keshin then back to Runa. "That would be improper. You are our lord's bonded, the lady of the house."

Runa wasn't surprised Miwa knew about their bond. Briefly Runa wondered if Keshin had written home about her, or if it was the gossipy soldiers who told her.

The thought was overshadowed by the second part of her statement. The suggestion that she, the nomadic healer, was the lady of *this* palace.

"Lady of the house?" The question fell from Runa's lips before she had a chance to censor herself.

Miwa smiled brightly and nodded. "Yes, my lady. It would be my honor to show you around the grounds. I'm sure my brother has business to attend to."

Keshin took Runa's hand, gently running his thumb along the sensitive skin on the back. "Go with Miwa. I'll see you at dinner."

For some reason, Runa thought Keshin would be the one showing her around their new home. Her heart felt like it was shrinking at the idea of being separated from him. Oh Aylis what was happening to her?

"Follow me, Lady Runa." Miwa led her inside.

Miwa was a flawless tour guide. Not only did she show Runa the palace, but she explained the history of the building and the lore connected with some of the decorative art pieces. Elegant, well spoken, and mild mannered, Miwa was exactly what Runa thought a lady should be. Everything that Runa was not—and feared she could never be.

Miwa led Runa from the central hall to a corridor of private chambers. "And these are your suites," Miwa said, opening the screen door.

The interior heavily featured wood features as well as the traditional straw mat floor covering. As her eyes swept over the bedroll that lay in the middle of the floor, the weight of the day settled in. Runa wanted nothing more than to curl up beneath the covers.

Unfortunately, there was no such reprieve as a line of servants entered the suites. They bowed to Runa, then to Miwa. One woman, who looked older than the rest of the serving women, stepped forward.

"Lady Runa, meet Hana, she is your head lady's attendant.

Hana bowed. "It is a pleasure to serve you, Iyashite,"

Runa fought the sigh that wanted to escape her lips. "Please call me Runa."

Hana's eyes widened as she looked at Lady Miwa, who graciously kept her face neutral. The attendant returned her gaze to Runa and bowed.

"Lady Runa, may we help you prepare for dinner?"

"Prepare?" Runa asked.

Hana nodded while Miwa held back a laugh that reminded Runa of the tinkling of bells. "This will be a grand dinner to welcome the Senshin home," Miwa said.

"Oh," Runa looked down at her traveling clothes. "I should probably clean up."

"The girls will draw a bath for you." Hana said, motioning toward another room.

The thought of a warm bath was tantalizing, it had been so long since she had gotten to soak in a tub instead of just cleaning up with buckets and rags.

But then another thought crossed her mind. "But I don't have anything to wear."

"I've arranged for some clothing to be delivered for you. We may have to make some last minute adjustments though," Miwa said.

Runa went to ask how they knew her size, but stopped when a sparkle of mischief danced behind Miwa's eyes. Runa decided not to question the woman and followed Hana into the bathing chamber.

Disrobing, Runa sunk into the warm embrace of water fragranced with oils and salts that washed away the day.

Chapter 11

Thoroughly bathed, Runa returned to the dressing room where Miwa had laid out a beautiful silk kimono. The base was a deep crimson color with embroidered overlapping circles that formed shining stars at the center. Her fingers trailed along Keshin's family crest on the back.

If anyone is worthy of wearing it, it's you, his words echoed in her mind.

It was the most beautiful thing she'd ever worn. As the women helped her dress, the silk slid over her skin like moonlight gliding across still water.

During her bath, Miwa left to prepare herself. When she returned, Miwa was dressed formally in a rich plum, and silver.

Miwa was fixing Runa's matching sash when she asked, "What is it like being bonded by the gods?"

The question threw her off guard. Nobody had ever asked her that before. "Excuse me?"

Runa felt Miwa's hands stop moving. "It's something that I will never experience. To know your soul has found the person the gods designed for you."

"Honestly, I never thought about it. I wanted nothing to do with your brother when we first met."

"The soldiers mentioned something about you summoning hellfire."

Runa's eyebrows furrowed. "That's not something I can do. I told him I would rather die than heal him."

Miwa covered her hand with her mouth. "I would have liked to see that."

"You still might."

"Good." When Runa gave her a confused look, Miwa continued, "He has people fawning over him all the time. It's good for him to have someone to humble him." Miwa took her hands. "I've always wanted a sister."

"We're not ... I mean ... he doesn't ... It's not ... like that."

"Oh, I didn't mean to assume. I thought the only thing missing was the ceremony."

There's a lot more missing, Runa wanted to say, but couldn't talk about her non-existent sex life with his sister.

Well, there was that kiss, but it was so brief, and Keshin hadn't given her any indication that he wanted another. When they shared a bed, his hands never wandered. Even though she saw the evidence of his arousal in the early morning.

Plenty of soldiers and officers laid with women from the village, but, to her knowledge, Keshin hadn't taken another woman to bed since they were bonded.

Miwa painted Runa's face, and styled her hair with a hairpin and a single ribbon before she declared Runa ready. Together they walked to the dining room.

Runa entered first and the room fell silent. Candles cast a warm glow on the woven tapestries hanging from the wood-paneled walls. The long tables were filled with men and women celebrating their lord's return home. Normally, she was used to people staring. But there was something about being in a room of Keshin's closest confidants and their families that made her uncomfortable. It was like every step she took was analyzed for fault or flaw.

She reminded herself that she was the Iyashite, she was chosen by the gods. There was only one other person in this room that was her equal. So she blocked them all out, everyone but Keshin.

He was draped in a luxurious looking black kimono embroidered with gold phoenixes to mirror her own. His formal attire was accented by a red haori jacket lined with black silk and fastened with his crest clasp in the front.

His eyes burned with heat unlike anything she had seen before, and Runa forgot how to breathe. Desire coursed through her body with each step she took closer to him. There was no question in her mind—she wanted him.

More than that, she had fallen in love with him.

She wasn't sure when her wariness became warmth, when irritation softened into curiosity. When had she stopped seeing Keshin as a sentence and started seeing him as a man?

Maybe it was the way he listened, even when she snarled. Maybe it was how he stood strong for her while she broke apart in front of him, offering no judgement, only presence. Maybe it was the way he carried the weight of his men, his land, the gods, without complaint.

Keshin didn't try to tame her. He didn't try to fix her. He simply stood beside her, unshaken, as if her storms were not something to survive but something worth walking into. And for all his power, for all the blood on his hands, he never once looked at her like she was fragile. He looked at her like he chose her. Not by the gods, but by him.

Runa knew little of love. Maybe it wasn't the sudden flare people spoke of in poems and songs. Maybe, for her, it was this, the slow burn of certainty. The ache in her chest when he allowed her to choose her fate and stood by her decision.

She wasn't choosing him because she was bound to him. Runa was choosing Keshin because, in his presence, she wasn't just the healer or the mark that bound them together, or the will of the gods.

For what felt like the first time in a while, she was just Runa, and that was enough.

Keshin stood and bowed to her, prompting the rest of the people in the room to do the same. Her heart fluttered at the sign of respect. When she reached the head of the table he straightened to greet her, then turned them both to present her to the room.

"My bonded, the Lady Runa, Iyashite of Aylis."

Cheers, hoots, and hollers congealed together in a collective cacophony. They were clapping for her, for them, for the future that they saw.

Keshin then pulled out the chair to his right, the place of honor, and waited for Runa to sit before retaking his own seat.

Miwa appeared, following the same path Runa took. She was greeted with respect and took the open seat next to Runa at the head of the table.

"It is good to see you, Lady Miwa," Hoshi said from his seat on the other side of Keshin.

Runa caught the corner of Miwa's mouth lift in a coy smile as she said, "I am glad for the army's safe return."

Their conversation cut short as the first course was served. Still, Runa watched as the two exchanged fleeting glances. Was that the barest hint of longing in the commander's eyes? And Miwa's sweet smile, was that just for him?

"Is the meal not to your liking?" Miwa asked.

There were multiple courses featuring fresh herbs, roasted lamb, honeyed root vegetables, and more rice than she'd ever seen at a meal before. It was a presentation of her favorite foods.

"It's delightful and it seems specifically curated."

"I'm not sure what you mean," Miwa said, lifting her cup to her mouth to take a drink.

That's how she wanted to play, then fine by Runa. She shifted in her seat, angling her body toward the men to her left.

Gathering a bite of meat in her chopsticks, Runa said, "It must take great skill to organize such a homecoming, wouldn't you agree, General?" Then she placed the bite of lamb in her mouth.

The second in command choked on his own bite of food, coughing into his napkin. Keshin, too, stopped mid-bite at the unexpected comment. Hoshi collected himself, sitting up straight before his gaze swept across Runa, fixating on Miwa.

"Such a person would be exceptional," he said.

The tips of Miwa's ears turned red. "Your words are kind, General."

Hoshi held her gaze a moment longer before returning to his food.

Miwa's piercing stare flicked back to Runa as she said, "Brother, how have you been sleeping at night? I know life on the road can be hard on you."

Now it was Runa's turn to blush. She hoped the cosmetics would conceal the color. It wasn't a secret that Keshin and she slept in the same tent. Keshin all but demanded it.

"I slept just fine, Sister," Keshin said, lifting his own cup to his mouth.

Runa's attention shifted from Miwa to Keshin as he raised a glass to his mouth. She stared at the column of his throat that moved as he took a drink, the way his tongue flicked out to capture stray drops of liquid on his lips.

She shouldn't be openly staring at him. Runa averted her eyes and shoved another bite of food in her mouth, chewing vigorously as if it could chase away the blush on her cheeks.

Miwa leaned in to whisper, "Worry about your own bed first, Sister, before you worry about mine."

"Well played, Sister," Runa said, the corner of her mouth lifting in a small smile.

Despite her embarrassment, something fluttered inside of her. Keshin said he had slept better since they started sharing a bed.

The rest of dinner passed with idle chatter until someone stood and recounted the duel between Keshin and Toraichi. He was a good storyteller, building up the tension with lilts in his voice and poignant pauses. He described how Hoshi ran Toraichi through before the vile man could run both the Iyashite and the Senshin through. As another round of cheers went up, Keshin stood and bowed toward his second. Hoshi did his best to hide the shock on his face as the room honored him.

"Neither I, nor my bonded, would be here without you, my friend. You've earned a boon from me."

"You honor me, my lord," Hoshi bowed to Keshin.

"The honor is mine," Keshin returned, placing one hand on Hoshi's shoulder. A moment of understanding passed between the two men. Keshin turned away from Hoshi and extended his hand toward Runa.

"Let us retire for the night."

Stuffed with one of the best meals she had in a long time, Runa nodded, placed her hand in his, and rose from the table. Wordless, they left the dining hall and returned to their chambers where servants had already rolled out the bed mat for them.

Runa's lead attendant, Hana, ushered her into a separate room so she and other attendants could divest Runa of her ornate kimono. She resisted the urge to comment about her ability to dress herself, but since it took two people to get into the garment, she doubted she could get out of it by herself. They dressed her in a simple nightgown.

Hana was the last to leave, giving Runa a knowing smile before she shut the doors. *What was she so happy about?* Runa wondered, standing before the sliding door.

For some reason, her body froze, as if it didn't want to take the step forward into the bedroom.

What was wrong with her? Why was she nervous to sleep next to Keshin? She had slept next to him—even naked—yet she was nervous now. Maybe it was all the talk at dinner. Or it could be the way Keshin made a show of presenting her to his people. She did not forget how Miwa called her the lady of the house.

The more she dwelled on it, the more she realized that the cause of her unease was her uncertainty of her place in Keshin's life now. It was a conversation long overdue for both of them.

Runa took a deep breath, attempting to settle her racing heart. When that didn't work she shook her arms, shimmed her shoulders, and rocked her head back and forth. That seemed to help get the jitters out. Summoning her courage, she opened the screen door and entered the room.

Keshin sat on the side of the mat closest to the door. He was dressed in a black robe, his hair unbound, falling freely around his face. Upon her entering, his head lifted to look at her. His eyes held the kind of peace that comes after a long storm, when soft sunlight breaks through the clouds.

Like Runa was his sun.

The speech Runa had been preparing disintegrated upon seeing him. Instead she blurted out, "How do you see me?"

"You are my bonded," Keshin answered, like that was all the explanation needed.

Her mouth turned down. That didn't sound like desire. But maybe, like so many other things between them, his meaning was lost in her translation.

"But what does that mean to you?" Runa asked, taking a single step and closing the distance between them.

"That the gods have blessed me."

That didn't make any more sense than his first answer.

"You are a man, not a god," Runa pinched the bridge of her nose.

"I am."

"And I am a woman."

"You are."

"Gods, can you be any more frustrating?" Runa stomped over to her side of the bed, laid down, and turned away from him, muttering, "Nevermind. Go fall on a spear."

Here she was, trying to put her heart on the line, and he didn't seem to care. Or worse, he didn't want her the same way she wanted him. That thought brought unexpected tears to her eyes. But she would not cry. She was the Iyashite. In the morning, she would ask for separate rooms.

But Keshin placed a hand on her side and rolled her over to face him.

"Runa, what are you asking?"

Her heart pounded as she sat up and placed her left hand on his chest. "Do you want me?"

Chapter 12

Sitting up, Runa couldn't maintain eye contact with Keshin. Instead she looked down to where her hands fidgeted with the fabric of her nightgown. Her heart continued to pound in her chest and her mouth felt parched, barren, her tongue thick and heavy. She swallowed and watched Keshin's eyes flick down to her throat, then back up to her mouth.

His hand cupped her face, forcing her to look at him and she felt like she could fly away from all the flutters in her stomach, or drown under the weight of her nerves.

Bringing her face closer to his, Keshin forced their eyes to meet. And in their depths Runa saw an inferno of desire.

"You are a beautiful woman Runa, and I've wanted you since the moment I saw you in my tent."

Something akin to a nervous laugh pierced the silence between their heartbeats. Runa knew people desired her for her powers. She didn't think this was part of his plan though. Maybe because she didn't think it would be true, didn't think Keshin would desire her in the same way she wanted him.

"That long?" Runa asked.

Keshin nodded. "From the first night, you've talked back to me, challenged me, irritated the fuck out of me. It took me time to realize it's part of the fire that burns bright inside of you, fueled by your passion to help others."

Runa's heart leapt with joy at his words and she went to draw him closer but he stopped her before she could press her mouth to his. Her golden eyes flicked to his, down to his mouth, then back up.

"But do you, Runa, desire me?" The pad of his thumb traced her jaw. "We are bonded by the gods but do you want to be with me as my wife?"

He was waiting for her, letting this be her choice. Runa couldn't deny the pull she felt towards Keshin, or the way heat pooled in her core at the thought of exploring his body for pleasure, something she had never done before.

Did she want to be his wife? She didn't have a good idea of what it meant to be a wife to someone. She didn't know if she could still be the Iyashite, and do her divine duty and be his wife at the same time. Yet, being with Keshin gave her a sense of security and a freedom to pursue her duty that she didn't have before him. He was patient with her, weathered the storms of her anger, and coaxed her back from the waters of the in between.

"I can't be locked away in your estate. It's not where I belong," Runa reached up to grab Keshin's hand.

"I would never ask that of you."

Her mouth fell open. He wouldn't ask her to remain at home. She really needed to stop making assumptions about this man.

"You'd let me travel with you?"

"I don't think you would let me leave you behind," Keshin said.

"Look, he can be taught," Runa said with a smile.

Keshin's thumb brushed over her lip. "Be sure this is what you want Runa. If you agree to be my wife, you'll be mine. And I will not let you go."

It was a bold statement with a possessive tone that Runa didn't know Keshin had.

"But you'll also be mine," Runa said. If she said yes, this man, in all his power and beauty, would be hers and hers alone.

Keshin nodded again. "We'll be bonded in all ways, not just by the gods."

Dozens of scenarios played out in her head, but in the end there was no question. Keshin was her equal here on earth, the one the gods designed especially for her. And she could not imagine a life without him.

There was no going back to before him.

Closing her eyes, Runa closed the rest of the distance between them, pressing her lips to Keshin's.

When she pulled away she whispered, "I want everything you have to give me. I want to be your wife, and for you to be mine."

Keshin cupped her face with both hands, guiding her lips back to his in a fervent kiss.

They had kissed once before, when Runa returned to the land of the living from the watery depths of limbo. That kiss was chaste, thankful, revering. This kiss was nothing like that.

Keshin met her intensity, mouth moving with hers like fire catching the wind, hungry, reckless, impossible to control.

"Tharaveld above," Keshin whispered against her lips between kisses. "I've been waiting for you for weeks."

"Why didn't you say anything?" Runa asked, her voice breathy and light like a petal carried on the wind.

"I was waiting for you. After your vitriol and the disdain you held for me, I knew things would have to be on your terms." Keshin peppered a trail of kisses from the corner of her mouth, along her jaw, to the sensitive skin behind her ear.

Each press of his lips on her skin fueled the knot of desire growing in her core. She had a hard time recalling her distant feelings when she had thought of Keshin as nothing more than a brainless brute.

"But I had hope that you'd come around. That someday I'd be worthy of you. That I'd get to kiss these luscious lips again."

Keshin kissed her again, guiding her down to the mat. Runa relished in every press of his mouth to hers, every teasing lick of his tongue against her lower lip, every nip of his teeth against the skin of her neck.

Her skin simmered with heat and longing, urging her to part her legs so his hips could settle between them.

It wasn't close enough though. She wanted to feel his skin on hers. Brazenly, she reached for the ties of his robe, undoing the knot and running her hands up his chest, over his shoulders, and down his arms to slide the garment off. Runa had seen Keshin shirtless numerous times, but this was different. She got to touch, taste, take pleasure from him in a way that no other woman would get to again.

"You're mine, Keshin," Runa muttered before placing a kiss to the beat of his heart calling to hers. She used his name, not his title.

As she did, Runa felt Keshin kiss the crown of her head. "My wife."

Runa had already chosen him when Keshin gave her a choice to go with Toraichi or stay with him. She fought the pulls of death to get back to him.

Keshin pulled her back into a fierce, dominating kiss, claiming her mouth like he would certainly claim the rest of her.

He found the hem of her nightgown and ripped the offensive garment right up the middle, tossing it aside like a fallen foe who had offended his ancestors.

Eyes laden with desire, Keshin's gaze roamed her lithe frame while his hands danced up her back and down her sides. Calloused hands palmed her breasts, gently squeezing and kneading before taking her already hardening nipples between his thumb and forefinger, rolling them and lightly pinching them. Jolts of pleasure shot right to her core. His touch was both comforting and stimulating.

Runa's hands traveled down the ridges of his back, feeling the corded muscle honed from years of combat.

In this moment, the rest of the world faded away and it was just the two of them.

Keshin lavished attention on her, swirling his tongue around the pebbled peak of her nipple before sucking it into his mouth, teasing it with careful bites. Switching to the other, he repeated his ministrations.

Runa's back arched into him as she wondered how she had never experienced pleasure like this before. The way his hands, mouth, and tongue coaxed pleasure out of her.

Fingers caressed the skin below her belly, traveling further south with each pass. There was a wetness between her legs and an unfamiliar pressure begging to be relieved. Keshin pulled at the ties of her undergarments, letting the fabric fall away from her body. He tossed it like he had disregarded her nightgown and stared unabashedly at her naked form.

Under his intense gaze, Runa felt the need to cover herself. He had seen her naked before, but this kind of intimacy made her want to hide from him. But he wouldn't let her. Keshin continued to kiss her as he ran a single finger over the top of her mound, testing her. And, Aylis,—she wanted more.

Keshin's finger dipped between her legs, into the slickness gathering there.

"So wet for me, my Iyashite. Has anyone ever touched you here?" Keshin said as he hovered over her.

A single finger circled her clit.

Runa gasped and involuntarily bucked her hips as a bolt of pleasure shot through her. Keshin gave a low chuckle and she wanted to swat him, but then he repeated the path. Again, he traced a path from her entrance to her clit. Her desire was replaced with her need for him to continue his exploration.

"Answer me," he demanded.

"No."

"No, what?"

"No one has ever touched me there."

"And no one else ever will," Keshin growled as he curled a finger into her core, stretching her and hitting a pleasure point inside of her. Breathing deeply, her chest expanded as she gasped then moaned his name. He was simultaneously relieving the building pressure, and driving it higher.

Withdrawing his finger, Keshin said, "There will be no one else. For either of us."

She wanted him to do that again, to push his finger into her, to stretch her core. Runa hated to admit it, but he could play her body like the strings of a shamisen. But even as she rocked her hips, seeking his finger, he denied her.

"Keshin," Runa pleaded.

"No one else, Runa."

"No one else," Runa vowed.

Her reward was Keshin lowering his mouth, but not to her lips. His head dipped between her legs and—ah! Keshin pressed his mouth to her hot center.

She had heard of performing this act, but the way they described it—Oh! Thoughts left her mind as he licked up her center. The tip of his tongue swirled around her swollen clit before he darted his tongue into her core again.

Runa's fingers entwined in his silky locks as he devoured her. Pleasure rocked through her, twisting her insides like the thread that bound them together.

When he slid his finger inside her and focused his tongue on her clit, Runa's body could take no more. She came apart as small spasms of pleasure rolled through her body.

Runa lay there panting as Keshin stood. Removing his own undergarments, Keshin's length sprang free. She'd seen enough male genitalia in her medical work to know that Keshin's cock was impressive, long and thick. How was it going to fit inside of her?

"I've never done this before," Runa blurted.

With a stroke of his hand on her cheek, he brought his forehead to hers. "There will be some pain but it will fade. We were made for each other."

Pressing a kiss to her lips, Keshin lowered himself to the cradle of her thighs. Runa felt him move the head of his cock through her wetness as he prepared to enter her. Once he was satisfied, he positioned himself at her entrance.

"Ready?" he asked.

"Yes," Runa said, curling her arms around Keshin's broad shoulders.

Keshin pushed in and Runa felt a strange combination of her muscles being stretched to the point of aching, but also satisfaction at being filled up.

"Breathe, Runa," he reminded her.

After a few more breaths, Keshin pushed in further. Each time she didn't think she could handle anymore, but her body adjusted to him. As Keshin said, the pain was fading away and she wanted him to—do something other than hold himself still inside of her. Runa moved her hips experimentally, taking his final inch.

"More," Runa begged, not knowing what for. She knew Keshin would be able to give her what she needed, though.

He withdrew and she lamented the loss of him, craving that delightful stretch of him filling her again. Runa didn't have to wait long for Keshin to slide back in with a shallow snap of his hips.

"Yes," Runa moaned, feeling full of him again.

She never knew joining with a man would feel this way. Or maybe it only felt this way because it was Keshin. The pleasure built inside her with each thrust of his hips.

Keshin balanced his weight on one powerful arm above her head and held her hip with the other.

"More," she whined.

"More what?" Keshin asked.

She wound her arms around his neck and pressed a kiss to the pulse there. "You."

He lifted one of her legs, bracing it on his shoulder as he began to drive deeper into her.

"You're mine, Runa," he said again, like he had so many times before. "Mine to love, mine to protect. You will wear my crest and sleep by my side. You will bear our children and our name."

Runa nodded frantically as he pounded deep into her. She wouldn't be the same after this. He would change her. They would be so much more than a bonded Senshin and Iyashite.

She was right on the edge of something building inside her, clouding her head. Keshin reached down to rub her clit once again and that was enough to send her over. A new type of pleasure ripped through her. Runa felt herself clench around Keshin's length as she cried out, clinging to him like he was her only anchor in this world.

But he wasn't done.

Keshin flipped her over, raising her hips to meet his own, and sheathed himself once again. This time, he was not as gentle as he snapped his hips against her. It was all she could do to take it.

Keshin snaked one arm around her torso, hand curving around her neck as he encouraged her to lean back against him.

"Give me one more," he growled in her ear.

Runa didn't think her body could do it. She already felt like a pile of melted wax from her last orgasm, but the hand bracing her hip reached down to the apex of her thighs and played with her clit again.

The pleasure spiked through her as Runa clenched around his cock. It was too much. Keshin still pounded her as hard and deep as possible.

"Take my cum," he said in a low gravelly voice.

"Yes." She wanted everything, every part of him melted into her skin, and to never let him go.

This orgasm rolled over her like a wind over the hills and she went limp against the mat. Two, three, more thrusts and Keshin's movements halted as he finished inside her.

Keshin pulled out gently and reached for a cloth in a small wash basin Runa had not noticed. Carefully he ran the cloth between her legs and up her core. Runa caught the red stain on the cloth as Keshin went to set it aside.

"Thank you," she said as Keshin gathered her against his body.

Their gazes met and Runa couldn't help but smile. Keshin looked at her as if she were the axis his universe spun around. He reached a hand up to trace her features.

"Sleep," he said. "Before I ravish you again."

Runa didn't know which one she wanted more.

Keshin's heartbeat echoed beneath her cheek, like a promise made just for her. Wrapped in his warmth, Runa realized she'd stopped searching because she found the one place she was always meant to be.

Epilogue
One Year Later

Morning unfurled gently over the estate, the mist lifting slowly from the tiled rooftops and manicured gardens. Koi stirred the still surfaces of their ponds with lazy ripples. The servants moved with quiet purpose, sliding doors open to let in the golden light.

Amidst it all, Runa stood on the packed earth of the rectangular practice ring. Nobody watched from the shaded overhang. This early in the morning, it was just her and Miwa. Not that Runa minded. She had been up most of the night, unable to sleep.

Runa's hands gripped the wooden practice naginata just like she had been taught. She worked with the spear and mastered it already, but this was a new type of weapon. One hand held the base, and the other was just above the center, ready to strike or pivot. She was partial to the polearm. Its length and curved blade, helped keep opponents at bay.

The hope was that she would never have to use it. But she never again wanted to be in a situation where she couldn't defend herself.

"What are you waiting for? Attack me," Miwa demanded.

Runa obliged, surging forward too fast, too eager. The blade whistled through the air as she threw her weight behind the strike. Muscle memory and instinct were just beginning to find their rhythm after training off and on for almost a year. She aimed toward Miwa's midsection.

The other woman rotated on her back foot, moving her body just enough to evade the strike. Miwa countered with her blade in a downward arc, catching the shaft of Runa's polearm near the base with a solid *thunk* that echoed throughout the space.

"Is that all you know how to do?" Miwa taunted.

"No," Runa gritted her teeth.

Shifting her weight, Runa twisted in a tight circle, striking again at Miwa's shoulder.

With calm precision, her mentor stepped into the strike, meeting Runa's upward arc with a firm crossblock. Runa held her naginata horizontally. The polearms clashed with a sharp crack that reverberated through Runa's arms. Her grip faltered and her fatigue from lack of sleep pulled at her limbs like weights.

"Your movements are slow, your body speaks before you act," Miwa said.

Runa's breath came shallow and fast, her muscles slow to respond as she tried to urge them into action. Frustration flickering in her chest when Miwa's strength held steady and her own felt like it was slipping through her fingers.

"You would be too if you were up all night," Runa grumbled.

"Who says I wasn't?" Miwa countered.

Runa backed up two steps, putting some distance between her and her opponent.

Miwa smiled. "Do I want to know why you were up all night? That hasn't happened since—"

Runa cut Miwa off before she could finish that thought. "I might as well inquire why you were up the night before your wedding?" Runa asked.

Miwa raised one manicured eyebrow as if to say, *you're not fooling me.*

Runa used the opportunity to press forward with a flurry of quick jabs, each one pushing Miwa back toward the edge of the training ring. Runa twisted, sweeping her naginata low. Her polearm cracked against the other woman's ankles, sweeping them out from under her. In a blur, Miwa was on her back.

Breathing heavily, Runa steadied her polearm in the dirt, giving it her weight as she looked down at her sister.

"Now who's distracted?"

"Not enough," Miwa said, sitting up. "But I'm proud of you. You weren't channeling Tharaveld, and you got one up on me."

Runa extended her hand to help pull Miwa up to her feet. "This is an interesting way to start your wedding day."

Something flickered in Miwa's features. The usual spark in her eyes dimmed. Her smile faltered at the edges. Then came that saccharine tone Runa knew Miwa used when she was pretending to be nice.

"Maybe this was imprudent of me." Miwa dusted the dirt from her clothes.

Runa pursed her lips. She didn't like this engagement and she certainly wasn't happy that Miwa was marrying Lord Shimada, no matter how proper he was.

Reaching across the space between them, Runa placed her hand on Miwa's shoulder. "You don't have to marry him."

Miwa looked at the hand on her shoulder, then back to her sister giving her a sad smile as she took Runa's hand in her own.

"Not all of us can marry for love," Miwa's voice quavered, tears threatening to spill from the corners of her eyes.

Runa's heart ached with quiet guilt. Love lived easy in her chest—but it hurt knowing Miwa would never know this kind of joy, not with the man waiting for her at the altar. But Miwa had heard Runa's protests time and time again. Still, the other woman would go through with this marriage. Grief for her sister curled around Runa's ribs.

"This isn't right."

Miwa held up one hand. "Our marriage will solidify a political and military alliance with Shimada's province."

Runa was going to respond, but a child's wail tore through the air, sharp, unrelenting. Instinctively, Runa passed her weapon to Miwa to stow and moved toward the sound.

Keshin stood, leaning against one of the wooden beams, their fussy, wiggly, three month old daughter in his arms. His hair was unbound and indigo robes strained against his bulk. With quick steps, Runa crossed the space to her husband and daughter.

"I'm sorry for interrupting," Keshin said.

"Or sorry you got caught eavesdropping?" Runa studied her husband's face to see the corner of his mouth raise almost imperceptibly.

"Good morning Hinari, did you want to start training too?" Runa cooed at the child. Taking her daughter into her arms, Runa bounced and soothed the babe until her cries ceased.

Of all the roles she imagined playing in her life, a mother had only ever been one that danced on the edge of her dreams. This tiny human was both a part of her, and part of the love of her life.

Hinari's tiny face smiled widely and she reached up with chubby arms to grab ahold of Runa's hair, yanking hard. Runa grimaced in pain as she coaxed her daughter to release the hair.

"Here," Keshin said, producing a small circular rattle.

She recognized it as the gift Hoshi had carved for her. Keshin dangled the toy above Hinari, who immediately snatched it and put it in her mouth.

Miwa appeared at Runa's shoulders, leaning over to caress Hinari's cheek. "She looks more like Keshin every day."

After carrying her for nine months, Hinari had the audacity to be the spitting image of her father. But as Runa looked into her child's eyes, she couldn't picture Hinari any other way. This was who she was meant to be. Whole, perfect, and theirs.

"She definitely has his lungs," Runa laughed.

"And her mother's sass," Keshin added with a pointed look at Runa.

"Gods help us," Miwa said.

Keshin turned his attention toward his sister. "Shouldn't you be preparing for your wedding?"

Color rose to Miwa's cheeks, but before she could speak, Runa said, "I asked her to spar with me."

It was a lie. Miwa had found Runa just as the sun was rising and asked to spar. She needed a distraction from her impending nuptials.

Keshin let out a sigh and shook his head as if he didn't believe a word Runa told him.

"Thank you Runa, but I think I've stalled long enough," Miwa said. She leaned down to press a kiss to Hinari's head before running a gentle hand over the fine hairs on the babe's head. "Your favorite aunt has to go take a bath and prepare herself for her new husband."

Runa's smile fell as she watched Miwa's retreating form. She said she was going to "prepare" herself, like she was a lamb to be sacrificed.

"This isn't right," Runa whispered so only Keshin could hear.

It wasn't the first time she'd objected to this marriage. But there was nothing she could do if Miwa agreed to marry Shimada.

"I have a feeling things will work out for her," Keshin said cryptically.

Runa's head snapped to her husband. "What do you mean?"

Reaching into his robes, Keshin produced a small scroll. "I received this from Isaku, on the front lines of Sakanoue."

That's the town where they met, the town where the remaining forces of Toraichi's army were trying to put down roots. Hoshi took the forces down there to handle the situation so Keshin could stay at home with Runa.

"This letter is from Isaku." Runa said.

Keshin nodded.

"If the letter is from Isaku then—"

Where was Hoshi?

Assessing her husband's face, his mahogany eyes lit with an inner glow, a twinkle of knowing.

Runa wanted to push further, to uncover what he was hiding, but a sudden wave of nausea crashed over her, pushing and twisting her stomach into knots and sending heat prickling up the back of her neck. The floor beneath her feet shifted, and she feared that gravity might claim her.

"Take her," Runa held out Hinari to Keshin.

He took their child without question, and Runa took off through the corridors of the estate toward their personal quarters. One hand was on her stomach, the other over her mouth, praying to Aylis she would make it to the bathing chamber.

Once there, Runa fell to her knees and emptied the contents of her depleted stomach. Somewhere in the back of her mind she registered that someone else had come in before a warm hand pressed to her back and gathered her hair away from her face. Keshin didn't say a word as the nausea worked its way out of her system. He simply moved his hand along her back in a soothing gesture.

If she were normal, it would be easy to blame her sickness on something she ate, or simply not feeling well. But, as the Iyashite, she did not get sick. Since developing her powers, the only other time she had felt nauseous was when she was early in her pregnancy with Hinari.

"Where is Hinari?"

"With her Uba."

Her stomach turned again, and she emptied the contents of her stomach.

"This is your fault," Runa tossed a glare over her shoulder.

Keshin cracked a smile and pulled Runa into his embrace. "I'll gladly accept responsibility."

"Feeling pleased with yourself?" Runa groaned, her throat burning.

He pressed a kiss to the top of her head. "Of course."

"You didn't need to answer that," Runa growled.

A part of her wanted to break away from his hold, to put as much distance between them as possible. But the warmth of his body soothed her fatigue. It was easy to relax into Keshin's hold.

With ease, he stood, cradling Runa in his arms as he returned to their bedchamber. Their bed mat was still out, which meant Keshin had ordered the servants to leave it. He must have been storming through their home to bring her back to bed.

Lowering her to the mat, Keshin pulled at the ties of Runa's training robes. Not in the way he did when he wanted to be inside her. That's what got Runa in this situation. This was the slow, methodical way he disrobed Runa when he wanted to take care of her.

And she let him.

When she was undressed and bundled under the covers, Keshin pulled her to him, one hand resting on her stomach. "You are with child."

Each spoken word reshaped their reality. Her body still remembered the ache of the last birth, the sleepless nights and tender days. And now, so soon, she would do it all again.

"Are you upset?"

Her hand came to rest over Keshin's, over the tiny life growing inside of her. She already loved this child.

"It's not that," Runa said.

But the weight of it settled over her like a stone sinking into her chest. A quiet tremble rippled through her. Not one of fear, exactly, but of awe, of fatigue, of the staggering realization that another would arrive before the first had barely learned to walk.

"I don't know if I'm ready to do this again."

"You don't have to be ready yet," Keshin said, voice low and steady. "You are not alone in this. Not now, not ever."

He brought her hand to his lips, brushing a kiss against her knuckles.

Runa lay tucked against Keshin's chest. The outside world may still spin, brewing storms yet to reach their shores—but here, wrapped in his arms, she only felt calm.

"You're not afraid?"

He pressed another kiss to her head, his voice barely a breath. "Not with you beside me."

Ahead, the unknown stretched wide. But with Keshin's hand in hers, Runa's fears were calmed. And in the silence that followed, the rise and fall of their breaths was a promise stronger than any blade. Whatever the world dared bring, they would face it as one.

Review Request

If you enjoyed reading this, please leave a review. I read every review, and they help new readers discover my books.

Amazon Page
Goodreads Page
Barnes & Noble Page

Acknowledgements

This novella seemed to materialize out of thin air. I had an image and a concept, a specific trope I wanted to write. It then grew that grew into something short and sweet.

As much as I poured myself into this novella, I was not alone.

First, thank you to my husband, Michael, who continues to faithfully support me in my efforts to pursue my writing dreams as I endeavor to make him a stay at home cat dad.

Thank you to my family for rooting me on, even if they didn't always understand.

This novel wouldn't be possible without Katelynn, Lauren, Zach, Frankie, Eliza, Sarah, and others who reminded me that this is a story worth telling.

Thank you to the industry professionals to help bring this story to life.

And thanks to you. Your support means more to me than you would ever know.

About the Author

Kelsey Winton writes nerdy love stories for readers who believe that romance is just as epic as any adventure. With a deep love for gaming, *Dungeons & Dragons*, and modern relationships, she blends heart, humor, and a little bit of chaos into every story. She lives with her partner and four feline overlords, who graciously allow her to write—when they're not demanding attention.

The Healer and the Warlord is a romantasy that proves even the fiercest bonds can be forged in choice, not just fate.

Connect with Kelsey on social media @authorkelseywinton or her website.

Also by

Love stories like this one? Kelsey Winton has more tales from the heart of a nerd waiting for you—packed with swoon, wit, and a little pixelated magic:

Games and Players Series

Games of Tangled Hearts
In this slow-burn, heartfelt, modern romance, Sylvie and Valentino try to turn their online connection into something real.